The Devil in the Flesh

Raymond Radiguet was born just outside Paris on 18 June 1903, the eldest of seven children and son of the illustrator Maurice Radiguet. At the age of fifteen he had his first and most significant love affair (which would later become the basis for *The Devil in the Flesh*) and abandoned his school studies. Soon established at the heart of the literary and artistic scene in Paris, Radiguet moved in circles which included Picasso, Modigliani and, most significantly, the avant-garde poet and film-maker Jean Cocteau. After Cocteau read some of the poems by this 'child with a walking-stick', he became convinced of Radiguet's genius and took him up as his protégé. Radiguet wrote *The Devil in the Flesh* while on holiday with Cocteau in 1921 and the novel was published in 1923. It was immediately a runaway bestseller, due in part to its author's age and its controversial subject matter, and its success allowed Radiguet to lead an increasingly lavish and bohemian lifestyle. In 1923, Radiguet contracted typhoid fever and died on 12 December, at the age of twenty. *Count D'Orgel's Ball*, his second novel, appeared posthumously in 1924, and a collection of his poetry was published the following year.

A. M. Sheridan Smith translated over fifty books from French, including works by Sartre, Lacan and Foucault, as well as writing novels and a biography of André Gide.

Robert Baldick was a translator, scholar and co-editor of Penguin Classics. His translations included works by Flaubert, Sartre and Verne, as well as a number of novels by Georges Simenon.

RAYMOND RADIGUET

The Devil in the Flesh

Translated by A. M. Sheridan Smith

Afterword by Robert Baldick

PENGUIN BOOKS

PENGUIN CLASSICS

UK | USA | Canada | Ireland | Australia
India | New Zealand | South Africa

Penguin Books is part of the Penguin Random House group of companies whose addresses can be found at global.penguinrandomhouse.com.

First published in France as *Le Diable au Corps* in 1923
This translation first published in Great Britain by Calder & Boyars Ltd 1968
Published in Penguin Classics 2011
3

Set in 11.25/14pt Dante MT Std
Typeset by Palimpsest Book Production Limited, Falkirk, Stirlingshire
Printed and bound in Great Britain by Clays Ltd, Elcograf S.p.A.

ISBN: 978-0-241-37261-6

www.greenpenguin.co.uk

Penguin Random House is committed to a sustainable future for our business, our readers and our planet. This book is made from Forest Stewardship Council® certified paper.

Contents

The Devil in the Flesh

One

I am sure to incur a good deal of reproach. But what am I to do? Is it my fault that I celebrated my twelfth birthday a few months before war was declared? The disturbance I experienced during that extraordinary period was probably of a kind never given to a boy of that age; but since nothing has the power to age us, despite appearances to the contrary, it was as a child that I had to conduct myself in an adventure that might well have disconcerted a man. I am not alone in this. My school-friends will retain a memory of that time quite different from that of their elders. Let those who are already reproaching me try to imagine what the war meant for so many of us very young boys – four years of holiday.

We lived at F., on the banks of the Marne.

My parents disapproved of friendships between the sexes. But our sensuality, which is born with us, though for a time it remains dormant, was aroused rather than quelled by their disapproval.

I have never been a dreamer. What appears dream to others more credulous than I seems to me to be as real as cheese to a cat – in spite of the glass that covers it. Yet the glass does exist.

If the glass breaks, the cat takes advantage, even if it is his master who breaks it and cuts his hand in the process.

Up to the age of twelve I had no sweetheart except a little girl called Carmen to whom I sent a love-letter by a younger boy.

Pleading love as my excuse, I took the liberty of requesting a meeting. She received my letter in the morning, before going to school. I had picked out the only girl with whom I had anything in common – she was clean and went to school with a little sister, just as I did with my younger brother. To silence these two witnesses I thought of pairing them off as well. To my own letter I therefore added another from my brother, who could not yet write, to Mlle Fauvette. I explained my plan to my brother and expatiated on our good fortune at finding two sisters of our own ages, endowed with such unusual Christian names. I had the misfortune to discover that I had not been mistaken as to Carmen's good breeding when, after lunching at home with my parents, who spoiled me and never scolded, I went back to school.

My class-mates were hardly in their desks – I, in my capacity as top boy, was stooping down to take out of the cupboard the books required for reading aloud – when the headmaster came in. The class rose to its feet. He had a letter in his hand. My legs gave way beneath me, the books fell and I set about picking them up as the headmaster talked to the teacher. The boys in the front rows were already turning round to look at my by now scarlet face because they had heard my name whispered. At last the headmaster called for me and as a subtle punishment, and also, he believed, to avoid putting mischievous thoughts into the minds of the other pupils, he congratulated me on having written a letter of twelve lines without a single mistake. He asked me if I had written it unaided, and requested me to accompany him to his office. We did not get so far. He reprimanded me in the school-yard, in the rain. What really disturbed my sense of morality was that he regarded with equal seriousness the fact that I had compromised the young lady's honour (her parents had sent him my declaration of love) and that I had stolen a sheet of writing-paper. He threatened to return this sheet to my parents. I begged him not to do so. He acceded to my pleas, but told me that he would keep the letter, and that if I ever did such a thing again he would no longer be able to conceal my ill-conduct.

This mixture of boldness and timidity in me puzzled and deceived my parents, just as my facility at school, which was really nothing more than laziness, gave me a reputation as a good pupil.

I returned to the classroom. In an ironical tone of voice the master addressed me as Don Juan. I was extremely flattered by this, especially as he was alluding to a work that was familiar to me but not to my class-mates. His 'Good afternoon, Don Juan' and my knowing smile transformed the attitude of the class towards me. Perhaps they already knew that I had got a boy from the junior school to take a letter to a girl. This boy was called Messager; I hadn't chosen him for his name, though to be frank it did strike me as being singularly appropriate.

At one o'clock I had begged the headmaster not to say anything to my father; at four, I was dying to tell him all about it. I was under no obligation to, of course; my confession could be ascribed to frankness. I knew my father would not be angry, so in actual fact I was delighted that he should learn of my prowess.

So I confessed, adding proudly that the headmaster and I had spoken in complete confidence (like two grown-ups) and that he had promised me that my secret would be safe with him. My father began to wonder whether I hadn't made up the whole of this love story from beginning to end, and went to see the headmaster himself. During their conversation he made a passing reference to what he could only imagine to be a childish prank. 'What!' exclaimed the headmaster, astonished and extremely annoyed. 'You mean he told you about it? But he begged me not to tell you! He said you would flay him alive!'

The headmaster told this lie in order to save face; for me it merely added to my self-esteem. It immediately won me the admiration of my class-mates and knowing winks from our teacher. The headmaster concealed his resentment. The poor fellow did not know what I knew: that my father had been so shocked by his handling of the affair that he had decided to take me away from the school at the end of the year. It was now the beginning of June. My mother, who did not want to spoil my chances of winning a prize, deferred the announcement until after the prize-giving. When the day finally arrived, I was the only pupil in my class to be awarded a gold medal. The headmaster, somewhat apprehensive as to the consequences of his lie, had tried to rectify his first mistake by another. His decision was unfair – the gold medal should, by rights, have gone to the same boy who had won the form-prize. It was also a miscalculation – the father of the boy who had won the form-prize also withdrew his son. The school thus lost its two best pupils.

Pupils such as us served as bait to attract others.

My mother thought I was too young to go to the Lycée Henri IV in Paris, by which she meant I was too young to travel by train. For two years I stayed at home and studied on my own.

I foresaw endless joys ahead of me. Since I was able to do in four hours what would have taken my former class-mates two days, I was left with more than half the day free. I walked alone along the banks of the Marne, which is so much 'our' river that my sisters would speak of the Seine as 'a Marne'. I even clambered into my father's boat, despite the fact that he had forbidden me to touch it. But I did not use the oars – and I never admitted to myself that I was afraid not just of disobeying my father, but simply afraid. I lay in the boat and read. In 1913 and 1914 I got through two hundred books. And not what might be called bad books; they might even have been considered the best, at least from a literary point of view, if not as training for a young mind. And later, at an age when adolescents are contemptuous of children's stories, I acquired a taste for their innocent charm – though at the time of which I speak nothing could have induced me to read them.

The disadvantage of this alternation of recreation and work was that it turned the whole year into an artificial holiday. My daily stint of work was little enough, but as I worked for less time than the others I also had to work when they were on holiday. This 'little enough' was for me the cork that a cat is made to carry at the end of its tail during its whole life, whereas it would probably prefer to have a saucepan for a month.

The real holidays were approaching, but they hardly concerned me since they would mean no change in my way of life. The cat was still looking at the cheese under the glass. Then the war came – and the glass was broken. The master had other cats to whip and the cat celebrated his good fortune.

Indeed, everyone in France was celebrating. The children, prize-books in hand, crowded in front of the posters. The bad pupils took advantage of the confusion in their families.

Every day, after dinner, we would go to the station at J., two kilometres from where we lived, and watch the military trains go by. We carried bunches of bluebells and threw them to the soldiers. Women in overalls poured red wine into their canteens, spilling litres of it all over the flower-strewn platform. I remember it all as being rather like a fireworks display. Never was so much wine wasted, nor so many dead flowers. At home we had to deck the windows with bunting.

After a while we stopped going to J. My brothers and sisters began to grow tired of the war; they thought it had gone on for too long. It stopped them going to the sea-side. They were used to getting up late and because of the war they had to get up at six o'clock to get the papers. And that didn't afford much amusement! But around the twentieth of August the hopes of these young monsters revived. After dinner, instead of leaving the table to the grown-ups, they stayed and listened to my father. He was talking about going away. But there would probably be no trains. They might have to travel a very long way by bicycle. My brothers teased my little sister. The wheels of her bicycle were only about fifteen inches in diameter. 'You won't be able to keep up. We'll leave you behind,' they said. My sister burst into tears. But what enthusiasm went into polishing and oiling those machines! Nothing was too much trouble. They even offered to repair mine. They rose at dawn to hear the latest news. There was general astonishment at this show of patriotism, but I discovered the real motives for it – a bicycle ride! All the way to the sea-side! And to a sea-side that was much further away and much more beautiful than the usual one. They would have burned down Paris to leave sooner. The terror of Europe had become their only hope.

But is the selfishness of children so very different from our own? In the country, in summer, we curse the rain, but farmers pray for it.

Two

A cataclysm is generally preceded by premonitory phenomena of some kind. The Austrian assassination and the storm over the Caillaux trial helped to spread an atmosphere that was particularly conducive to extravagance. Similarly, my first real memory of war preceded the war itself.

It happened like this.

My brothers and I used to make fun of one of our neighbours, a grotesque-looking dwarf of a fellow with a white goatee-beard and a cowl. He was called Maréchaud and was a local councillor. Everyone called him Old Maréchaud. Although he lived only next door we refused to acknowledge him when we saw him. Naturally enough this made him extremely angry and one day, unable to contain himself any longer, he rounded on us in the street: 'So we don't say good morning to a councillor any more, eh?' We turned tail and ran. From that moment it was open war between us. But what could a local councillor do against us? On their way to and from school my brothers rang his bell. They were further emboldened in this by the fact that they had little to fear from the dog, who must have been as old as I was then.

The day before the Fourteenth of July 1914, as I was going out to meet my brothers, I was astonished to see a crowd of people gathered in front of the Maréchauds' front gate. Their house was clearly visible at the end of a garden behind a few well pruned lime-trees. Apparently their young maid had gone mad and taken refuge on the roof. She had been there since two o'clock in the afternoon and refused to come down. Appalled by the scandal, the Maréchauds had closed their shutters. This of course emphasized the tragic appearance of the mad girl on the roof, since the house looked deserted. People were shouting abuse at her employers for doing nothing to rescue the unfortunate young woman. She was staggering about over the tiles, although she didn't seem to be drunk. I would have liked to stay and watch, but our maid called us in. Mother said it was time we got on with our homework. If we didn't come soon we wouldn't be allowed to stay up for the celebrations. I went, inwardly cursing my misfortune and praying that the maid would still be on the roof when I went to meet my father at the station.

To my great relief she was still there, but the few people who passed on their way home from Paris were hurrying back for dinner so as not to miss the ball. They spared her only a brief glance and moved on.

In fact, as far as the maid was concerned, the whole afternoon had been nothing but a semi-public rehearsal. She was to make her début in the evening, in the usual way, with the Fourteenth of July illuminations as her footlights. She had not only those in the street but also those in the garden: despite their feigned absence, the Maréchauds had not dared to leave their garden unilluminated. Their position in the community demanded it. The fantastic aspect of this house of crime – on the roof of which, as on the deck of a dressed ship, a woman was pacing up and down, her hair floating in the wind – was considerably enhanced by the voice of the woman herself. It was guttural, almost inhuman and yet strangely gentle: it gave me gooseflesh to hear it.

The firemen of a small district as ours were 'volunteers', and had other business to attend to besides fires. So if there did happen to be a fire, the dairyman, the pastry-cook and the locksmith would come round at the end of their day's work and put it out, if it had not by this time gone out of its own accord. Since the call-up, our firemen had also formed themselves into some mysterious kind of militia that effected exercises, manoeuvres and watch patrols. At last these worthies arrived on the scene and made their way through the crowd.

A woman came forward. She was the wife of a councillor – who happened to be an ardent opponent of Maréchaud. For some time she had been loudly bewailing the lot of the poor creature on the roof. She began giving the chief fireman instructions: 'Treat her gently. Try to win her over with kindness. It's what she is probably most in need of. The poor child can't have known much happiness in that house. They beat her, you know. And if she's afraid of being dismissed, if it's the fear of losing her job that has made her act in this way, tell her that I'll take her on myself and double her wages.'

This noisy expression of charitable sentiments drew a poor reception from the crowd. The woman was getting tiresome. What they wanted to see was a good chase over the roof. The firemen, six in number, climbed over the railings, surrounded the house and mounted their attack on all sides. But no sooner did one of them appear on the roof than the crowd, like children at a Punch and Judy show, began to bawl and shout, warning the victim of his approach.

'Be quiet!' cried the councillor's wife. But this merely provoked more shouts of 'There's one! There's one!' from the audience. Hearing these cries, the demented creature on the roof began to arm herself with tiles and aimed one straight at the helmet of the first fireman to reach the top. The other five came down at once.

While the shooting-galleries, roundabouts and booths on the

main square were complaining of the poor attendance – especially since this was a night when the takings should be particularly heavy – the more adventurous of the local lads had clambered over the railings and into the garden in order to get a better view of the show. I cannot remember what the mad creature said, but she spoke in the resigned, deeply sorrowful tones of someone who knows she is in the right and that everyone else is in the wrong. The local lads, who preferred this spectacle to the fair, wanted nonetheless to enjoy both. So, terrified lest the girl should be caught while they were away, some of them ran off to have a quick go on the roundabouts. The others, doubtless the less turbulent element, installed themselves on the branches of the lime-trees, for all the world as if they were watching the military review at Vincennes, and contented themselves with letting off a few Bengal lights and bangers.

One can imagine the feelings of the Maréchauds, locked up in their house in the midst of all this light and noise.

The councillor – the husband of the charitable lady – had climbed up on to the low wall that supported the railings and was delivering a speech about the infamous behaviour of the girl's employers. He was duly applauded.

Thinking that it was meant for her, the mad girl acknowledged the acclamation of the crowd. But she still had a pile of tiles under each arm and did not hesitate to throw one whenever a helmet appeared over the edge of the roof. In her wild inhuman voice she thanked the crowd for having understood her at last. She made me think of some female corsair captain alone on her sinking ship.

The crowd, having grown a little tired of the spectacle, was beginning to disperse. I wanted to stay with my father; my mother could go off with the children and satisfy their need to feel sick on the roundabouts and the Big Dipper. In fact, I felt this strange need more strongly than did my brothers. I loved to feel my heart quicken to a new, irregular rhythm. But the deeply poetic quality of this spectacle satisfied me more. 'You look quite pale,' said my mother. I found a ready excuse in the Bengal lights. 'They make you look green,' I said.

'All the same, I'm afraid it'll upset him,' she told my father.

'Oh, no one could be less sensitive,' said my father. 'He can stand anything – except seeing a rabbit being skinned.'

My father said this so that I could stay. But he knew that I was upset. I sensed that it had upset him too. I asked him to lift me up on to his shoulders so that I could get a better view. In actual fact I was about to faint; my legs were giving way beneath me.

There were now not more than about twenty people left. The bugle sounded for the torchlight tattoo.

Suddenly a hundred torches shone on the mad girl. It was as if, after the soft glow of the footlights, the flood-lights had been turned on to photograph a new star. At that moment, thinking perhaps that the end of the world had come, or simply that she was about to be caught, she made a last gesture of farewell and threw herself off the roof. She fell through the glass roof of the porch, causing a terrible din, and landed on the stone steps. So far, I had tried to bear up to everything that had happened, though my ears were ringing and my heart was about to fail me. But when someone called out, 'She's still alive', I fell unconscious from my father's back.

When I finally came to he took me down to the Marne. For a long time we lay in the grass in silence.

As we passed the house on our way back, I thought I saw, between the railings, a white shape – the ghost of the maid! But it was only Old Maréchaud in his night-cap, inspecting the damage to his porch, his roof, his flower-beds, his blood-stained steps and his good name.

If I have dwelt at some length on this episode it is because, more than any other, it represents for me the strange period of the war, and because it shows how I was affected less by the picturesque than by the poetic side of things.

Three

Gunfire could be heard. There was fighting near Meaux. It was said that some uhlans had been taken prisoner near Lagny, fifteen kilometres away. Hearing my aunt speak of a friend of hers who had fled in the first days of hostilities, after burying her clocks and several tins of sardines in her garden, I asked my father how we could take our old books with us. I was more concerned about them than anything else.

But just as we were getting ready to leave, we read in the papers that it was all quite useless.

My sisters now began going to J. to take baskets of pears to the wounded. They had found some compensation, though a rather poor one it is true, for the collapse of all their fine plans. By the time they got to J. the baskets were almost empty!

I was supposed to be going to the Lycée Henri IV, but my father decided to keep me at home for another year. My only diversion during that gloomy winter was to run to the newsagent to make sure that I got a copy of *Le Mot*, a magazine I was particularly fond of, which came out on Saturdays. As a result, I never got up late on Saturdays.

But spring came round again and my days were enlivened by new pranks. Several times that spring, under the pretext of collecting money, I went out with a young lady. Wearing our Sunday best we set out, I holding the collecting-box and she the basket of flags. On the second occasion my colleagues showed me how to make the best of these days off that were so conveniently enhanced by female company. From then on we collected as much money as we could in the morning, handed it to the lady organiser at midday and spent the whole afternoon playing on the hills of Chennevières. For the first time I had a friend. I liked to go collecting with his sister. For the first time I got on well with a boy who was as precocious as I. I admired his handsome looks and his temerity. We were further bound together by our common contempt for the other boys of our age. Only *we* were capable of understanding things; and, moreover, we alone were worthy of women. We regarded ourselves as men. As it happened, we were not going to be separated. René was already at the Lycée Henri IV and I was to join him there in his class, the Third.* Originally, he was not going to take Greek; but he now made the very great sacrifice of persuading his parents to allow him to take it after all. In this way we would stay together throughout our time at school. As he had not taken it in his first year he had to have private lessons. René's parents were completely baffled by this sudden change of heart; only the year before he had begged them not to make him do Greek and they had reluctantly agreed. They saw it in fact as a result of my good influence and, whereas they no more than tolerated their son's other friends, they positively approved of me.

For the first time in my life I was never, for a single day, at a loose end during the holidays. I realized that no one can be older than his years, and that my precarious contempt for others had melted like snow as soon as someone had deigned to take notice of me in the way I wanted. The progress we

* In French lycées the classes are numbered from one to eight, the Eighth Class being the most junior.

made together halved the journey our separate prides would have had to make.

On the first day at school René acted as an invaluable guide.

With him everything became a pleasure and, whereas alone I was incapable of taking a single step, I now enjoyed every minute of the twice-daily walk between Henri IV and the Bastille station, where we caught our train.

Three years passed in this way, with no new friendships and with no greater pleasure to look forward to than our Thursday* spent together in the company of girls – René's parents innocently invited their son's and their daughter's friends to tea together, thus providing us with excellent introductions. We won small favours, and they were won of us, under the pretext of a game of forfeits.

* In France the lycées are closed on Thursdays and open on Saturdays

Four

With the return of fine weather my father liked to take my brothers and myself out for long walks. One of our favourite outings was to Ormesson, which we reached by following the course of the Morbras, a river that was little more than a yard wide. We walked through fields where there grew a flower that you would find nowhere else and whose name I have forgotten. Clumps of watercress and mint concealed the water's edge. In spring the river bore away thousands of white and pink petals. It was the hawthorn blossom.

One Sunday in April 1917, we took the train to La Varenne which was the usual starting-point of our walks to Ormesson. My father said that at La Varenne we would be meeting some very nice people, the Grangiers. I knew of them because I had read the name of their daughter, Marthe, in the catalogue of an exhibition of paintings. One day I heard my parents saying that a M. Grangier would be visiting us shortly. He came, clutching a portfolio containing works by his eighteen-year-old daughter. Marthe was ill. Her father wanted to give her a surprise by getting her watercolours included in a charity exhibition that was being organized by a committee of which my mother was president. There was nothing original about these watercolours; they were quite obviously the work of a conscientious pupil in an art class; one could just see her sticking out her tongue and licking her brush.

When we arrived at La Varenne the Grangiers were waiting for us on the platform. M. and Mme Grangier must have been about the same age, in their late forties. But Mme Grangier looked the older of the two; because of her short figure and inelegant appearance I took an instant dislike to her.

In the course of that walk I was to notice that she often frowned and her forehead would be covered with wrinkles that took about a minute to disappear. So that I might have every possible excuse for disliking her, without having to reproach myself with being unfair, I hoped she would talk in a vulgar way. In this she was to disappoint me.

The father seemed a good enough fellow, an ex-army sergeant, probably very popular with his men. But where was Marthe? My heart fell at the prospect of a walk with no other company than that of her parents. But she would be coming on the next train, in a quarter of an hour. 'She wasn't ready in time,' Mme Grangier explained. 'She'll be coming with her brother.'

When the train drew into the station Marthe was standing on the footboard of the carriage. 'Wait for the train to stop,' shouted her mother . . . I was delighted by the girl's daring.

Her very simple dress and hat showed how little she cared for the opinion of strangers. She was holding by the hand a little boy who looked about eleven. It was her brother: a pale sickly-looking child with an albino's hair.

We set off, Marthe and I in the lead. My father walked behind, between the Grangiers.

My brothers looked bored by their new, puny little companion, who was not allowed to run.

I complimented Marthe on her watercolours, but she replied modestly that they were only studies. She attached no importance to them. She would show me much better things she had done, like her 'stylized' flowers. As this was our first meeting I thought it better not to say that I considered such flowers to be ridiculous.

She could not see me very well under her hat. But I was observing her carefully.

'You don't look very much like your mother,' I said.

It was intended as a compliment.

'Yes, people sometimes say that. But when you come to our house I'll show you some photographs of mother when she was young. You'll see how much I take after her.'

I was very saddened by this reply and prayed that I would not see Marthe when she was her mother's age.

Wishing to overcome my disappointment at her distressing reply, and failing to understand how it could be distressing only for me, since Marthe fortunately did not see her mother with my eyes, I said:

'You shouldn't do your hair like that. Straight hair would suit you better.'

I was suddenly terrified at what I had said. I had never spoken to a woman like that before. I thought of what my own hair looked like.

'You'd better ask mother about it,' she said. (As if she needed to make any excuses!) 'Usually I do my hair quite well, but I was late already and I was afraid I'd miss the second train. Anyway I didn't intend taking my hat off.'

What sort of a girl was she, I thought, to allow a boy of my age to criticize her hair?

I tried to find out what her literary tastes were. I was pleased that she had read Baudelaire and Verlaine and delighted at her reasons for liking Baudelaire, though they weren't mine. I detected in them signs of a rebellious spirit. Her parents had finally agreed to tolerate her tastes. But Marthe was angry with them because they had done so only out of parental fondness. In his letters her fiancé talked of what he was reading; but although he advised her to read certain books, he also forbade her to read others. He had forbidden her to read *Les Fleurs du Mal*.

I was unpleasantly surprised to learn that she was engaged, but delighted to know that she disobeyed a soldier who was silly enough to be afraid of Baudelaire. I felt, with some pleasure, that he must often shock Marthe. After the first unpleasant surprise I was delighted at this narrow-mindedness on his part, especially as I feared that, had he too liked *Les Fleurs du Mal*, their future home might have been like the one in *La Mort des Amants*. I then asked myself what business this was of mine.

Her fiancé had also forbidden her to attend art classes. Though I never attended them myself, I offered to take her with me, adding that I often went along to a very good art school. But fearing that my lie might be discovered, I begged her not to say anything about it to my father. He did not know, I explained, that I often missed the gymnastics lessons in order to go to the Grande-Chaumière. For I did not want her to think that the reason I was afraid of my parents knowing was that they did not want me to see naked women. I was happy to let it remain a secret between us and, shy as I was, I already felt I had her in my power.

I was also proud that she preferred me to the country, for so far she had made no reference to the scenery. From time to time her parents would call out: 'Look Marthe, over there on the right. Aren't the Chennevières hills beautiful!' Or her little brother would come up and ask her the name of a flower he had just picked. She took just enough notice of them to avoid making them angry.

We all sat down in a meadow near Ormesson. I now regretted that my candour had led me to go so far and to precipitate things rather too quickly. If I had spoken to her in a less forward manner, I thought, if I had acted more naturally, I might now have been able to dazzle Marthe with my conversation and win the esteem of her parents by expatiating on the history of the village. I refrained from doing so. With good reason, it seemed to me, for after all that had been said between us, a conversation so entirely unconnected with our common anxieties would have broken the charm. I believed that something very serious had taken place. In fact, it had, although it was not until later that I knew, because Marthe had misunderstood our conversation in the same way as I had. At the time, I was unable to see this. I knew that what I had said to her had a very definite significance. But I thought I had declared my love to someone incapable of understanding it. I forgot that M. and Mme Grangier could quite easily have heard everything I had said to their daughter; but would I have been capable of saying it in their presence?

'It's not because I'm afraid,' I repeated to myself. 'It's only her parents and my father that are stopping me from leaning over and kissing her.'

But deep inside me another boy was only too pleased that such a barrier existed.

'What a good thing I'm not alone with her,' he thought. 'For I'd be just as afraid to kiss her and would have no excuse for not doing so.'

Which is how the timorous deceive themselves.

We took the train back from Sucy. As we had a good half-hour to wait we sat down at a café terrace. I had to endure Mme Grangier's compliments. They humiliated me. They reminded her daughter that I was still a schoolboy and would be taking my *baccalauréat* in a year's time. Marthe wanted a grenadine; I ordered the same. That same morning I would have been ashamed to be seen drinking grenadine. My father looked surprised. He always let me order aperitifs. I was afraid he might tease me for being such a good boy. He did, but in such a subtle way that Marthe never guessed that I ordered a grenadine merely because she had done so.

At F. we said goodbye to the Grangiers. I promised Marthe

that the following Thursday I would bring her all my copies of the magazine *Le Mot* and also *Une Saison en Enfer*.

She laughed. 'Another title my fiancé wouldn't approve of!'

'Come now, Marthe!' said her mother, frowning. Such expressions of insubordination always shocked her.

My father and brothers had spent a rather boring day. But what did I care! Happiness is selfish.

Five

On Monday morning, at the lycée, I felt no desire to tell René, to whom I usually confided everything, about the events of the previous day. I was in no mood to be laughed at for not having given Marthe a clandestine kiss. But something else surprised me: René no longer seemed so very different from my other friends.

My love for Marthe had dispossessed René, my parents and my sisters.

I fully intended making an effort of will not to see her before Thursday, the day on which we had arranged to meet. But on Tuesday evening I could wait no longer, and in my weakness found many excellent reasons for taking the book and the magazines round to her after dinner. Marthe would see in this impatience the proof of my love for her, I told myself, and if she did not, I would find ways of making myself clear.

I ran like a madman to her house and arrived in a quarter of an hour. Then, fearing that I might disturb her during dinner, I waited for ten minutes, bathed in sweat, in front of her gate. I thought that this delay would give my palpitations time to stop. Instead, they got worse. I almost turned round and went home again, but for some minutes a woman had been looking at me curiously from a neighbouring window, wondering no doubt what I was doing there hovering outside the gate. She made up my mind for me. I rang the bell. I entered the house. I asked the maid if Madame was at home. Almost immediately Mme Grangier appeared in the small room into which I had been shown. I jumped, which made it appear as if I had intended the maid to understand that when I asked for 'Madame' I had really meant 'Mademoiselle'. Blushing, I begged Mme Grangier to excuse me for disturbing her at such an hour – as if it had been one o'clock in the morning – but as I would be unable to come on Thursday, I had brought the book and the magazines for her daughter.

'How very convenient,' said Mme Grangier, 'because Marthe wouldn't have been able to see you on Thursday anyway. Her fiancé is home on leave a fortnight earlier than expected. He arrived yesterday and Marthe is dining tonight at his parents'.'

So I left, and since I was sure I would never see Marthe again I tried hard not to think about her, with the result that I thought of nothing else.

However, one morning a month later, as I was getting off the train at Bastille station, I saw her getting out of another carriage. She was going to the shops to buy various things for her new home. I asked her if she would walk with me as far as Henri IV.

'Oh, do you go there?' she said. 'Next year, when you're in the Second Class you'll have my father-in-law as geography master.'

I was annoyed that she should talk to me about school as if it was the only subject of conversation suitable for someone of my age, and replied rather bitterly that that would be quite amusing.

She frowned – reminding me of her mother.

We were coming to Henri IV, and not wishing to leave her on what I considered to be a wounding note, I decided to go into class an hour later, after the art period. I was pleased to see that Marthe did not disapprove of my decision, or reproach me in any way, but rather seemed grateful that I should make such a sacrifice for her. In fact, of course, it was no such thing. And I was grateful that in exchange she did not suggest that I should accompany her on her shopping expedition, but that her time would be at my disposal as I had put mine at hers.

We were now in the Luxembourg Gardens; the Senate clock struck nine. I decided to miss school altogether. Miraculously I had more money in my pocket that morning than a schoolboy usually has in two years, as I had sold my rarest postage-stamps the day before at the stamp market behind the Puppet Theatre on the Champs-Elysées.

In the course of our conversation Marthe had mentioned that she was lunching with her future parents-in-law. I decided to persuade her to stay with me. Half-past nine struck. Marthe gave a start – she had not yet got used to the idea of someone's renouncing all his scholastic duties for her. But seeing that I had not moved from my iron chair, she did not have the nerve to remind me that I ought to have been sitting at my desk in the lycée.

So we stayed as we were. Happiness must be like this. A dog jumped out of the pool and shook himself. Marthe stood up, like someone who had just woken from an afternoon sleep and was shaking off her dreams. She started doing gymnastic exercises with her arms, which I did not regard as very propitious for our relationship.

'These chairs are too hard,' she said, as if to excuse herself for standing up.

She was wearing a silk dress and it was rumpled where she had been sitting. I couldn't help imagining the pattern that the iron bars of the chair must have made on the skin beneath.

'You'd better come with me to the shops, since you've decided to play truant,' said Marthe, referring for the first time to what I had abandoned for her.

We visited several lingerie shops and I managed to stop her ordering things that she liked and I didn't. For example, I stopped her choosing pink, which I hate, and which was her favourite colour.

After these initial victories I had to persuade Marthe not to lunch with her future parents-in-law. Thinking that she would be unable to lie to them for the simple pleasure of remaining in my company, I tried to find something that would persuade her too to play truant. She very much wanted to go to an American bar, but had never dared to ask her fiancé to take her to one. Besides, he didn't know any bars. Here, I thought, was my chance. Her refusal was stamped with such genuine disappointment that I thought she would in fact come. After half an hour, however, having tried in every way I could think of to persuade her, and having finally admitted failure, I accompanied her to her parents-in-law's house. On the way I felt like the condemned man who hopes right up to the last moment that something will happen to save him. I saw us getting nearer and nearer to the street and still nothing happened. But suddenly Marthe knocked on the window and stopped the taxi-driver in front of a post office.

'Wait here a minute,' she said. 'I'll go and telephone my mother-in-law and tell her that I'm at the other end of Paris and can't get there in time.'

A few minutes passed and I grew more and more impatient. I then noticed a flower-stall nearby. I got out and bought some red roses, which I chose one by one and had made up into a bunch. I was thinking not so much of how pleased Marthe would be with them, as the fact that she would have to tell another lie that evening, in explaining to her parents where the roses had come from. Our secret plan, formulated at our first meeting, of attending classes at an art school; the lie on the telephone, which she would have to repeat that evening to her parents, and to which must be added the lie about the roses – these were for me favours more sweet than a kiss. For I had often kissed girls on the lips and had not found it particularly pleasurable. I forgot that this was because I had not loved them, and as a result, I had no great desire to kiss Marthe. Whereas this complicity between us was a quite new experience.

Marthe emerged from the post office smiling. After the first lie she looked radiant. I gave the taxi-driver the address of a bar in the rue Daunou.

Marthe was in ecstacies. She behaved for all the world like a boarding-school girl being taken out for the day, talking excitedly about the barman's white coat, the graceful way he shook the cocktail-shaker and the strange or poetic names of the various mixtures. From time to time she smelt the roses and promised that she would do a watercolour of them which she would give me as a souvenir of that day. I asked her to show me a photograph of her fiancé. I thought he looked handsome enough. But sensing already the importance she attached to my opinions, I was hypocritical enough to say that he was very handsome, but in such a way as to give her the impression that I was not very convinced and was saying so only out of politeness. This, I thought, would plant a seed of doubt in her mind, and at the same time win me her gratitude.

But in the afternoon we had to turn our attention to the purpose of her visit. She knew her fiancé's tastes and he had left the task of choosing their furniture entirely to her. Her mother had at first insisted on going with her. Marthe had finally persuaded her not to and promised not to do anything silly. She had come into Paris that day to choose some furniture for their bedroom. I was determined to show neither extreme pleasure nor extreme displeasure at anything Marthe said, but I had to make a great effort to keep my pace steady now that it was no longer in step with the rhythm of my heart.

I regarded having to accompany Marthe on this expedition as a singular misfortune. I was to help her choose a bedroom for her and another man! Then I saw how I could choose a bedroom for Marthe and myself.

I forgot her fiancé so quickly that after a quarter of an hour I would have been quite surprised if someone had reminded me that another than I would sleep beside her in this bedroom.

Her fiancé liked the Louis Quinze style.

Marthe's bad taste drew her in a quite different direction: she inclined rather towards the Japanese. So I had to fight on two fronts. Speed of movement was the essential. When Marthe said something that suggested that she might like a certain piece, I immediately suggested its opposite, which I didn't necessarily like myself. In this way it seemed that I was giving in to her caprices when I abandoned my first choice for another that displeased her less.

She murmured: 'And to think that he wanted a pink bedroom!' She no longer dared to admit her own tastes, but attributed them to her fiancé. I guessed that in a few days we would both be laughing at them.

Yet I did not understand this weakness. 'If she doesn't love me,' I thought, 'what possible reason can she have for giving in to me, sacrificing her own tastes and those of her fiancé to mine?' I could think of none. The simplest explanation was still that Marthe loved me. Yet I felt sure that she didn't.

'At least let's leave him the pink material,' she said. Let's leave him! These words alone were almost enough to make me loosen my hold. But leaving him the pink material was tantamount to giving in completely. I explained to Marthe that pink walls would spoil the effect of the simple furniture 'we had chosen' and, at the risk of going too far, suggested that she should simply have the walls of her bedroom white-washed!

This was the crowning blow. All afternoon Marthe had been

so browbeaten that she took it without flinching. She simply said: 'Yes, I think you're right.'

At the end of this exhausting day I could justifiably congratulate myself on my achievements. Item by item, I had succeeded in transforming this marriage of love, or rather of infatuation, into a marriage of reason, and a strange marriage of reason at that, since reason had no part in it, each finding in the other only the advantages provided by a marriage of love.

As she left me that evening, far from seeking to avoid further advice, she had asked me if I would help her during the next few days to choose the rest of her furniture. I said that I would, but only if she swore that she would never tell her fiancé, since the only chance of his coming in the end to accept this furniture was for him to think that it was entirely her own choice. Then, if he really loved Marthe, what gave her pleasure would also please him.

When I got home my father looked at me as if he had already learned of my escapade. He knew nothing, of course; how could he?

'Oh, Jacques will soon get used to the room,' Marthe had said. As I lay in bed I said to myself that if she thought about her marriage before going to sleep, she must have a quite different idea of it that night than she had done before. For my part, whatever the outcome of this idyll might be, I had well and truly prepared my vengeance on her Jacques: I was thinking of their wedding night in that austere room, 'my' room!

The next morning I looked out for the postman. As I had anticipated, he had an absentee note for my father. I took the mail, threw the other letters into our letterbox and put the note from the lycée in my pocket. This was too simple a trick not to use it again.

Missing school meant, to me, that I was in love with Marthe. But this was not so. In fact Marthe was only an excuse to play truant. The proof was that, having tasted the pleasures of freedom in Marthe's company, I wanted to enjoy them alone, and even initiate others into the same pleasures. Freedom soon became a kind of drug.

The school year was drawing to a close, and I saw with horror that my idleness was to remain unpunished. I wanted something dramatic, like expulsion from school, to close this period of my life.

If we live constantly with the same ideas, if we see only one, passionately desired object, we become unaware of how criminal are our desires. Naturally I had no wish to cause my father distress; yet I desired the very thing that would distress him most. School had always been a torture for me; Marthe and freedom had made it quite intolerable. I was well aware that if I liked René less it was because he reminded me of the lycée. The thought that the following year I might find myself once again among the puerilities of my school-friends made me physically ill.

Unfortunately for René I had got him to share my vice too often. So when he announced to me that he had been expelled from Henri IV, I felt sure that I must have been expelled as well. I would have to tell my father, for he would prefer me to tell him myself, before the letter from the lycée arrived. This letter would be too serious to dispose of as I had the others.

It was a Wednesday. The next day, the holiday, I waited for my father to leave for Paris and told my mother. The prospect of four days of upset in the family alarmed her more than the news itself. I then set out for the bank of the Marne where Marthe had said she might meet me. She was not there, which was just as well. I would have drawn strength of the wrong kind from our meeting, and used it against my father. As it was, the storm broke after a day of empty misery and I returned suitably downcast and chastened. I arrived home slightly after the time I knew my father would normally be there. He would 'know' by now. So I wandered about the garden, waiting for him to call me in. My sisters were playing very quietly. They guessed something was wrong. One of my brothers, excited by the storm, told me to go in and see my father, who was lying down in his room.

Shouts and threats would have allowed me to rebel. But it was much worse than that. My father said nothing at first; then, without a trace of anger, his voice even gentler than usual, he said:

'Well, what are you going to do now?'

The tears that would not come from my eyes hummed in my head like a swarm of bees. To his will I could have opposed my own, however weak. But before such gentleness I had no thought but submission.

'Whatever you want me to do.'

'No, don't lie to me any more. I've always let you do as you like. You'd better continue that way. I suppose you're determined to make me regret it.'

When one is very young one is too inclined to think, as women do, that tears make up for everything. My father did not even expect tears. Confronted with this generosity, I was ashamed of the present and of the future. For I felt that whatever I said would be a lie. 'At least let this lie give him some comfort,' I thought, 'before becoming a new source of pain to him.' No, not that; I am still trying to lie to myself. What I wanted was something that would be hardly more tiring than taking a walk and which, like walking, would leave my mind free to dwell without interruption on Marthe. I pretended that I wanted to paint and had never dared to say so. Once again, my father did not say no; on condition that I continued to learn at home what I would have learned at school, I would be allowed to paint.

When the ties between two people are not yet firm, a single meeting missed is sufficient to lose sight of the other. Through thinking of Marthe so much, I thought of her less and less. My mind was reacting in the same way as one's eyes react to the wallpaper in one's room. Through seeing it so often, they cease to see it at all.

More remarkable still, I even began to enjoy my work! I had not lied as I had feared.

When some quite external thing made me think more attentively of Marthe I did so without love, with the sadness that one feels for something that might have been. 'No, no. Too good to be true,' I told myself. 'You can't choose your bed *and* lie in it.'

Six

One thing surprised my father. The letter from the lycée never came. It was this that caused him to lose his temper with me for the first time. He thought that I had intercepted the letter, then pretended that I was owning up in order to obtain his forgiveness. In fact, there was no such letter. I thought I had been expelled from the lycée, but I was wrong. So my father was even more baffled when, at the beginning of the summer holidays, we received a letter from the headmaster.

In it he asked if I was ill and whether I was to be entered for the next school year.

Seven

The joy of pleasing my father at last helped to fill the emotional void in which I now found myself. For if I thought that I no longer loved Marthe, I at least regarded her as the only person who would have been worthy of my love. Which amounts to saying I still loved her.

Such was the state of my emotions when, one day at the end of November, a month after receiving an announcement of her wedding, I found on my return home an invitation from Marthe that began: 'I cannot understand your silence. Why don't you come and see me? Have you forgotten that it was you who chose our furniture?'

Marthe lived in J.; her street went right down to the Marne. There were no more than a dozen houses on either side. I was surprised that hers was so big. In fact she only occupied the upper floor; the owners and an old couple lived below.

When I arrived for tea it was already dark. The only sign of life was the light of a fire coming from one of the upstairs windows. Seeing the irregular shadows thrown by the flames like waves against the window, I thought the room must be on fire. The iron garden-gate had been left open. Such carelessness surprised me. I looked for the bell, but couldn't find one. So I ran up the three steps leading to the front door and knocked on one of the ground-floor windows, on the right, from where I could hear voices. An old woman came to the door. I asked her where Mme Lacombe lived (this was Marthe's new name). 'Upstairs,' she said. I walked up the stairs in the dark, stumbling and bruising myself, terrified that something dreadful had happened. I knocked. Marthe herself opened the door. I almost threw my arms around her neck, as strangers do after being saved from a shipwreck. She would not have understood. She must have thought that I was behaving rather strangely, for the first thing I said was: 'Why is there a fire?'

'While I was waiting for you I made an olive-wood fire in the drawing-room and I was reading by it.'

As I entered the little room that served as her drawing-room I saw that although it was not over-furnished, the wallpaper and the thick carpets – which were as soft as fur – had the effect of reducing it almost to the dimensions of a box. I felt both pleased and disappointed, like a dramatist who is watching his play for the first time and realizes his mistakes too late.

Marthe was lying in front of the fire again, poking the embers and taking care not to let any of the charred wood fall into the ash.

'Perhaps you don't like the smell of olive-wood? My parents-in-law had it sent to me from their estate in Provence.'

Marthe seemed to be apologizing for adding a detail of her own to this room that was my work. Perhaps this one thing introduced a discordant note into some overall plan that she did not fully understand.

On the contrary, I was delighted with the fire and amused to see that, like me, she liked to wait until she was burning on one side before turning over. Her calm, serious face had never seemed more beautiful than in this wild light. By not spreading out into the whole room, the light preserved all its strength. As soon as one moved away from it one was in darkness, knocking oneself against the furniture.

*

Coquetry was quite foreign to Marthe's nature. Even her playful moods were invested with a certain gravity.

As I sat with her my mind became quite dulled. She seemed different. Now that I was sure I no longer loved her, I was beginning to do so. I felt incapable of all those calculations and machinations which I had always thought, and still thought, were a necessary adjunct to love. I suddenly felt a better person. This change would have opened anybody else's eyes but mine; but I failed to see that I was in love with Marthe. On the contrary, I interpreted it as a proof that my love was dead and was to be replaced by friendship. The prospect of such a friendship made me realize how wicked any other feeling would have been, wronging as it would a man who loved her, to whom she belonged and who was unable to be with her.

Yet there was something else that should have shown me the true state of my feelings. Some months before, when I used to meet Marthe, what I thought to be my love for her did not prevent me from judging her, from finding ugly most of the things that she found beautiful, and most of the things she said childish. Now if I did not think as she did I felt I was in the wrong. After the coarseness of my earlier desires I was unable to recognize this new, deeper feeling of tenderness. I no longer felt capable of carrying out what I had promised myself. I was beginning to respect Marthe, because I was beginning to love her.

I went back every evening; I did not even think of asking her to show me her bedroom, let alone whether Jacques liked our furniture. I wished for nothing more than this eternal engagement, our bodies lying side by side in front of the fire, touching each other, and I not daring to move, lest a single gesture on my part should destroy my happiness.

But Marthe, who also felt the magic of those hours, thought she was alone in doing so. She interpreted my blissful laziness as indifference. Thinking that I did not love her, she felt that I would soon tire of this silent room if she did nothing to bind me to herself.

We lay there in silence. This was proof to me of my happiness.

I felt so close to Marthe, so sure that we were thinking of the same things at the same time, that it would have seemed absurd to speak, like talking to oneself when one is alone. But the poor girl was intimidated by this silence. It would have been wiser of me to make use of those crude means of communicating that are speech and gesture, even while regretting that no more subtle means existed.

Seeing me every day sink deeper and deeper into this delicious silence, Marthe imagined that I was becoming more and more bored. She was ready to do anything to please me.

She liked going to sleep in front of the fire with her hair unpinned. Or rather I thought she was asleep. In fact, her sleep was only an excuse to put her arms around my neck. Then she would wake up, her eyes moist with tears, and say that she had had a sad dream. She would never tell me what it was. I took advantage of her feigned sleep to breathe in the smell of her hair, her neck, her burning cheeks, no more than brushing them with my lips so as not to wake her. Such caresses are not, as is commonly believed, the small change of love, but on the contrary its highest denomination, which only passion can afford. For myself I thought they came within the permitted bounds of friendship. And yet I began to fear that it is only love that gives us rights over a woman. I could quite well do without love, I thought, but I could not bear never to have any rights over Marthe. And in order to assure my rights I was even prepared to love her, though I regarded such a course as regrettable. I desired Marthe, but did not understand my desire.

As she slept, her head on my arm, I leaned over to look at her face, which was surrounded with flames. I was playing with fire.

One day, as I approached too close, though our faces were not touching, I was suddenly like the needle which, having once moved a fraction of an inch beyond the mark, is in the magnet's power. Is it the fault of the magnet or the needle? I became aware that my lips were on hers. Her eyes were still closed, but she was quite obviously not asleep. I kissed her, amazed at my boldness, whereas in fact it was she who had drawn my head towards her mouth. Her hands clung to my neck; they would not have held me so fast in a shipwreck. And I did not understand whether she wanted me to save her or to drown with her.

She was sitting now, holding my head in her lap and stroking my hair, repeating very gently: 'You must go away and never come back.' The tears welled up inside me. Each time one fell on Marthe's hand I expected her to cry out. I blamed myself for breaking the spell. I told myself that I must have been mad to place my lips on hers, forgetting that it was she who had kissed me. 'You must go away and never come back.' Tears of anger mingled with my tears of pain, just as the fury of the captured wolf causes him as much agony as the trap. If I had spoken it would have been to abuse Marthe. My silence worried her; she took it as a sign of resignation. With perhaps a kind of far-sighted injustice I interpreted her thoughts as: 'Since it is too late for us anyway, I am quite glad that he should suffer.' I shivered in front of that fire; my teeth chattered. To the real pain that was dragging me out of childhood were added childish feelings. I was like a theatre-goer who will not go home because he doesn't like the way the play ends. 'I won't go away,' I said. 'You've been making fun of me all along. I don't want to see you again.'

For, although I did not want to go home, neither did I want to see Marthe again. I would rather have driven her from her own home.

'You're only a child,' she sobbed. 'Don't you understand? It is because I love you that I ask you to go.'

I answered spitefully that I was well aware that she had certain duties and that her husband was at the Front.

She shook her head: 'I was happy before I met you. I thought I loved my fiancé. I forgave him for not understanding me very well. It was you who showed me that I didn't love him. My duty is not what you think it is. It is not that I musn't lie to my husband, but that I mustn't lie to you. Go away and don't think I'm being unkind. You'll forget me soon enough. I don't want to be the cause of unhappiness in your life. I'm crying because I'm too old for you!'

This avowal of love was the most sublime childishness. And whatever emotions I experienced subsequently, nothing could be quite like the delightful feeling at seeing a nineteen-year-old girl cry because she thought she was too old.

Like the first taste of a strange fruit, my first kiss had been something of a disappointment. We derive our greatest pleasures not from novelty but from familiarity. A few minutes later I had not only grown accustomed to Marthe's mouth – I could not do without it. And then she spoke of depriving me of it for ever.

That evening Marthe walked home with me. To feel myself closer to her I huddled under her cape and put my arm around her waist. She no longer said that we must not see each other again; on the contrary, she was sad because we would have to part in a few minutes. She made me swear a thousand foolish things.

When we got to my house I didn't want to let Marthe go back alone, so I accompanied her home again. This childish nonsense could no doubt have gone on for ever, for she wanted to go back with me again. I agreed on condition that she only came half-way.

I arrived home half-an-hour late for dinner. It was the first time. I blamed the train. My father pretended to believe me.

*

My body had lost all weight. In the street I walked as lightly as in my dreams.

Up until then, everything I had coveted as a child I had had to do without. Moreover, the presents I did receive were spoilt by having to thank people for them. How much a child would value a present that gave itself! I was drunk with passion. Marthe was mine; and it wasn't I who said so, but she. I could touch her face, kiss her eyes, her arms, dress her, hurt her; she was mine. In my ecstacy I bit her in places where her skin was exposed, so that her mother would suspect that she had a lover. I would have liked to mark her with my initials. In my childish savagery I rediscovered the ancient significance of tattoos. Marthe said: 'Yes, bite me, mark me. I want everyone to know.'

I would have liked to kiss her breasts. I dared not ask her, thinking that she would offer them herself as she had offered her lips. After a few days, when I had grown familiar with her lips, I could imagine no greater delight.

Eight

We would read together by the light of the fire, into which she often threw the letters that her husband sent her every day from the Front. Judging by their frequent expressions of anxiety I guessed that Marthe's letters to him were becoming less and less tender and less and less frequent. It was not without a certain disquiet that I watched those letters burn. For a second the fire became much brighter; the truth was I was afraid to see more clearly.

Marthe would often ask me if it was really true that I had loved her ever since our first meeting, and reproached me for not telling her before she was married. Had I done so, she said, she would never have married Jacques. For although at first she had felt a sort of love for him, it had diminished as the period of their engagement became longer and longer on account of the war. By the time she married Jacques she no longer loved him at all. She had hoped that her feelings would change during the fortnight's leave Jacques had been given.

He was clumsy. The one who loves always annoys the one who does not. And Jacques loved her more than ever. His letters showed that he was unhappy, but that he held his Marthe too highly in his esteem to believe that she would be capable of infidelity. He blamed only himself, begging her to tell him what he had done to offend her; 'I feel so coarse when I am with you. I feel everything I say hurts you.' Marthe replied simply that this was not so and that she had nothing to reproach him with.

It was now the beginning of March. Spring was early. On the days when Marthe did not come with me into Paris she was waiting for me in the evening on my return from art school. Naked beneath her dressing-gown, she lay in front of the fire. Olive-wood from her parents-in-law's estate burned in the hearth. She had asked them to renew her supply. I do not know what held me back. Perhaps it was simply the fear of doing something one has never done before. I was reminded of Daphnis. But in this case it was Chloe who had been given one or two lessons and Daphnis did not dare to ask her to teach him. Besides, I tended to regard Marthe as a virgin, given over during the first fortnight of her marriage into the arms of an unknown man, who had taken her several times by force.

Alone in my bed at night I spoke Marthe's name, furious with myself – I who regarded myself as a man – for not being man enough to make her my mistress. Each time I went to see her I swore that I would not leave until she was.

On my sixteenth birthday, in March 1918, she gave me a dressing-gown like her own. She hoped I would not be angry but she wanted to see me try it on there. I was so happy that I nearly made a pun; something I never did. My *toga praetexta*, my pretext! For I realized that what had inhibited me was a sense of the ridiculous, of feeling dressed when she was not. At first I was going to put the dressing-gown on that same day. Then, blushing I saw what a reproach this present implied.

Nine

From the beginning Marthe had given me a key to her flat so that I would not have to wait in the garden if she happened to be delayed in town. It occurred to me that I could use this key for less innocent purposes. It was Saturday. When I left Marthe I promised I would come and lunch with her the following day. But I had decided to go back that evening as early as possible.

At dinner I told my parents that René and I were planning to go for a long walk in the forest of Sénart the next day; I would have to leave the house at five o'clock in the morning. Since the entire household would still be asleep, no one would know what time I had left, and if I had slept out.

As soon as my mother knew of our proposed outing she insisted on preparing a picnic basket for us herself. This was most disconcerting; it would utterly destroy the sublimely romantic nature of my act. Whereas before I had been looking forward to Marthe's fright on seeing me enter her bedroom, I now imagined her peals of laughter as Prince Charming appeared with a shopping-basket on his arm. I told my mother that it was quite unnecessary, that René had everything we needed, but to no avail. She would not hear of it. So I said no more; further resistance would only arouse suspicion.

One man's misfortune, however, may be the source of others' happiness. As my mother filled the basket that spoiled my anticipation of my first night of love, I noticed the envious eyes of my younger brothers. I thought of secretly giving them the basket, but even at the risk of a sound thrashing they would have told the whole story – once they had eaten everything – for the sheer pleasure of seeing me caught out.

Since no way of disposing of the contents seemed safe enough, there was nothing to be done but resign myself to taking the basket.

I had sworn to myself that I would not leave before midnight, so as to be sure that my parents were asleep. I tried to read. But when the town hall clock struck ten, and my parents had already been in bed for some time, I could wait no longer. My parents' bedroom was on the first floor. Mine was on the ground-floor. I had left my boots off so that I could climb over the wall as quietly as possible. With them in one hand and the basket, which contained breakable bottles, in the other, I carefully opened a small door at the back of the house. It was raining. Good! I thought. The rain will deaden the noise. When I saw that the light was still on in my parents' room I almost went back to bed. But having gone so far I could not bear to go back. I had to put my boots back on, of course, because of the rain. I then had to climb over the wall, so as not to make the bell on the gate sound. I had already taken the precaution, after dinner, of placing a garden chair against the wall to facilitate my escape. This wall was surmounted by tiles, which the rain had made very slippery. As I was hoisting myself up, one of the tiles fell off. In my terror the noise seemed to be magnified tenfold. I now had to jump down into the street. I held the basket between my teeth and jumped. I landed in a puddle. For a full minute I stood there, my eyes fixed on my parents' window. Had they heard? Neither of them came to look. I was safe!

To get to Marthe's I followed the Marne. I was hoping to hide my basket in a bush and collect it the next day – no easy matter in wartime. And sure enough, at the only spot where there were any bushes and where it was possible to leave the basket, was a sentry guarding the J. bridge. I hesitated for a long time, more nervous than a man laying a stick of dynamite. Eventually I managed to hide the food.

The gate of Marthe's house was locked. I took the key that was always left in the letter-box and let myself in. I crossed the garden on tip-toe and walked up the steps to the front door. Inside I took off my boots and climbed the stairs.

Marthe is so nervous! I thought. She might even faint when she sees me coming into her room. My hand was shaking; I couldn't find the keyhole. At last I found it and turned the key slowly in the lock so as not to wake anybody. In the hall I bumped into the umbrella-stand. I was terrified of pressing bell-pushes instead of light-switches, so I groped my way to the bedroom. Suddenly I stopped in my tracks; I felt an overwhelming desire to run away. Marthe might never forgive me. Or supposing I discovered that she was being unfaithful, and found her with a man!

I opened the door and whispered: 'Marthe?'

She answered: 'You might have waited until tomorrow morning instead of giving me such a fright. You got your leave a week early, then?'

She thought I was Jacques!

I was pleased with the way she would have welcomed him; I was less happy that she should have hidden something from me. So Jacques was coming home in a week's time!

I switched on the light. She stayed facing the wall. It would have been simple enough to say 'It's me', and yet I didn't say it. I kissed her neck.

'Your face is wet,' she said. 'Go and dry yourself.'

She turned round and gave a startled cry. Her attitude changed from one second to the next. Without appearing to need any explanation for my presence there at night, she said:

'My poor darling, you'll catch a chill! Get undressed at once.'

She ran off to revive the fire in the sitting-room. When she came back she saw that I hadn't moved.

'Shall I help you?'

I had feared this moment more than anything else, feeling that I would make myself ridiculous. Now, thanks to the rain, the act of undressing had taken on a maternal significance. But Marthe went out again to the kitchen to see if the water for my toddy had boiled. At last she found me naked on the bed, half covered by the eiderdown. She scolded me: I was mad to stay naked. I should have rubbed myself with eau de cologne.

Marthe went over to the wardrobe and took out some pyjamas. 'They should be your size.' Jacques' pyjamas! And I thought how possible it was – after all, Marthe had thought I was he – that he might arrive on the scene at any moment.

I was now in bed. Marthe joined me. I asked her to put out the light. For even in her arms I was afraid of my own shyness. The darkness would give me courage.

'No,' Marthe replied gently. 'I want to watch you go to sleep.'

These charming words rather embarrassed me. They were a perfect expression of the touching understanding of this woman who had risked everything to become my mistress and, knowing nothing of my chronic shyness, was now prepared to let me go to sleep beside her. For four months I had been saying that I loved her, and I had not yet given her the proof which men are generally so prodigal with, and which they frequently offer in the place of love. I turned off the light myself.

I now felt the same anxiety I had experienced before entering Marthe's flat. But like my hesitation before the door, my hesitation before love was short-lived. Moreover, my imagination promised itself such pleasures as it was no longer able to conceive of. For the first time, too, I was afraid of being like the husband and leaving Marthe with an unpleasant memory of our first moments of love.

As a result of all this she was much happier than I. But my anxiety was amply rewarded by the sight of her marvellous eyes the moment we untwined from each other's arms.

Her face was transfigured – so much so that I was surprised that I could not actually feel the halo that surrounded her face, as in religious pictures.

Relieved of my fears at last, I found others taking their place.

For I began to understand the power of an act that my shyness had prevented me from performing until then. I was now afraid that Marthe might belong more to her husband than she had led me to believe.

I find it impossible to appreciate anything the first time I experience it. So my enjoyment of the pleasures of love was to increase each day.

But meanwhile this first, false pleasure brought with it a man's pain – jealousy.

I blamed Marthe because the expression of gratitude on her face taught me the value of physical ties. I cursed the man who had aroused her body before me. I saw how stupid I had been to think of Marthe as a virgin. At any other time to desire the death of her husband would have been little more than a childish piece of wishful thinking; it now became almost as criminal as killing him. I owed my newfound happiness to the war; I hoped the war would now complete its task. It must commit the crime for me, like a hired assassin.

We were now crying together, but they were tears of happiness. Marthe reproached me for not having prevented her marriage. But had I done so, I reasoned, I would not now be in this bed that I had chosen. She would be living with her parents and we would be unable to see each other. She would never have belonged to Jacques, but she would not belong to me either. Without him, she would have had no basis for comparison and, hoping for something better, she might have had doubts about me. I did not hate Jacques. I hated the knowledge that we owed everything to the man we were betraying. But I loved Marthe too much to regard our happiness as a crime.

We cried because we were like weak, helpless children. If I abducted Marthe, because she belonged to no one but me I would simply lose her. For we would be separated. We were already thinking of the end of the war which would also be the end of our love. We knew that. It was useless for Marthe to swear that she would leave everything and follow me. I am not rebellious by nature and, putting myself in Marthe's place, I could not see myself taking such drastic steps. Marthe explained why she thought she was too old for me. In fifteen years life would still be just beginning for me, and women of the age that Marthe was now would be in love with me. 'It would only make me unhappy,' she added. 'If you left me, I should die. If you stayed, it would be out of weakness and I would suffer to see you sacrificing your happiness.'

In spite of my indignation I was angry with myself for not appearing to be sufficiently convinced of the contrary. But Marthe needed little convincing and my poorest reasons were enough for her.

'Yes, I hadn't thought of that,' she answered. 'I know now that you're telling the truth.'

Confronted by Marthe's fears, I felt a good deal less confident in myself. My arguments were weak and it seemed as if I was offering them only out of politeness. 'Don't be silly. How could you think such a thing?' I said. But I was too well aware of the attractions of youth not to realize that I would leave Marthe when her youth was beginning to desert her and mine was still at its height.

Although my love seemed to me to have attained its definitive form, it was really only beginning. It weakened at the slightest obstacle.

The follies that possessed our minds that night tired us more than those of our bodies. Whereas the first seemed to provide a respite from the second, in fact they merely exhausted us further. Cocks were crowing – there seemed to be a great many of them. They had been crowing all night. I realized that it was a poetic lie that cocks crow only at dawn. This was hardly surprising: insomnia was unknown to me at that age. But Marthe noticed it too, and her surprise was such that it must have been for the first time. She could not know why I suddenly held her so tightly in my arms. Her surprise had proved to me that she had never spent a night awake with Jacques.

My fears made me regard our love as something quite exceptional. We think we are the first to experience such anxieties, not realizing that love is like poetry, and that all lovers, even the most ordinary, imagine themselves to be innovators. When I said to Marthe – I did not believe it, but wanted her to think that I shared her anxieties: 'Later on, other men will attract you and you'll leave me,' she assured me that she would always be mine. For my part, I gradually persuaded myself that I would stay with her, even when she was no longer so young. My laziness led me to base our eternal happiness on her energy.

Sleep had taken us by surprise in our nakedness. When I woke and saw that she was uncovered, I was afraid she might have got cold. I felt her body. It was hot. Seeing her asleep like that gave me immeasurable pleasure. After ten minutes the pleasure became unbearable. I kissed her shoulder. She did not wake. A second, less innocent kiss had the effect of an alarm-clock. She started up and, still rubbing her eyes, began to cover me with kisses, like somebody one loves and finds in one's bed after dreaming that he is dead. On the contrary, she thought she had dreamt that I was there, and then had found me there when she awoke.

It was already eleven o'clock. As we were drinking our chocolate, the bell rang. I immediately thought of Jacques; 'I hope he has a gun on him.' Though so afraid of death, I did not flinch. On the contrary, I wouldn't have minded if it had been Jacques so long as he killed us. Any other solution would have been too ridiculous in my eyes.

Envisaging death calmly is valid only if one envisages it alone. Death in the company of the beloved is no death, even for unbelievers. The painful thing is not to leave life, but to leave whatever gives it meaning. When love is one's life, what is the difference between living together and dying together?

I had no time to think of myself as a hero. When it occurred to me that Jacques might kill only one of us, I measured my egotism. Did I even know which would be worse, Marthe's death or mine?

As Marthe did not move I thought I must have been mistaken and that the bell had rung in the flat below. But it rang again.

'Keep quiet! Don't move!' Marthe whispered. 'It must be my mother. I'd completely forgotten she was coming round after Mass.'

I was happy to witness one of her sacrifices. When a mistress or a friend is a few minutes late at an appointment, I start imagining they are dead. Attributing such imaginings to Marthe's mother, I gloated over her fears, and over the fact that it was I who was responsible for them.

After a confabulation below (obviously Mme Grangier asking the landlord if he had seen her daughter that morning), we heard the garden gate close once more. Marthe looked out through the shutters and said: 'Yes, it was her.' I couldn't deprive myself of the pleasure of seeing Mme Grangier walk off, missal in hand, obviously worried by her daughter's inexplicable absence. She turned round once more towards the closed shutters.

Ten

Now that I had nothing more to desire I felt how unfair I was becoming. It worried me that Marthe could lie so unscrupulously to her mother and I was hypocritical enough to hold it against her. Yet love, which is a form of selfishness involving two selves instead of one, sacrifices everything to its own interests and lives off lies. Driven on by the same demon, I then reproached her for concealing from me her husband's arrival. Until then I had repressed my despotic instincts on the grounds that I had no proprietary rights over Marthe.

My callousness sometimes abated. 'Before long you won't be able to bear the sight of me. I treat you just as badly as your husband,' I moaned.

'My husband doesn't treat me badly,' she replied.

I returned to the attack. 'Then you're betraying both of us. Say you love him. Don't worry – in a week's time you'll be able to betray me with him.'

She bit her lip and burst into tears: 'What have I done to make you so cruel? Please, don't spoil our first day of happiness!'

'You can't love me very much if this is your first day of happiness,' I snapped.

Blows like this hurt the giver more than the receiver. I did not believe what I was saying; yet I felt a need to say it. I couldn't explain to Marthe that my love for her was increasing. It had no doubt reached the awkward age and these bitter attacks were the growing pains of love turning into passion. It became more than I could bear and I begged Marthe to forgive my harsh words.

Eleven

The landlord's maid slipped some letters under the door. Marthe picked them up. There were two from Jacques. 'Do what you like with them,' she said, as if in answer to my doubts. I was ashamed. I asked her to read them to me, but keep them for herself. Acting on one of those impulses that drive us to the worst extremes of bravado, Marthe tore through one of the envelopes. It was difficult to tear – the letter must have been a long one. Her action became a new occasion for reproach. I hated this bravado – and the remorse that it would not fail to cause her. Not wanting her to tear up the second letter, I controlled my feelings. This scene had taught me that Marthe was not the sweet-natured girl I had taken her for. At my request she read the letter. She had torn up the first letter on impulse, but it was not impulse that made her exclaim after glancing through the second: 'Heaven has rewarded us for not tearing up this letter. Jacques says that all leave has been suspended in his sector. He won't be home for another month.'

Only love could forgive such a lapse of taste.

This husband began to annoy me more than if he had been there and I had had to take care not to cross his path. A letter from him began to take on the importance of a ghost. We lunched late. About five o'clock we went out for a walk by the river. Marthe was astounded when, under the very eye of the sentry, I took out a basket from a clump of grass. She was very amused to hear how it got there. I was no longer afraid of appearing ridiculous. We continued walking, our bodies clinging to each other, our fingers intertwined, quite unaware of the unseemliness of our behaviour. It was the first sunny Sunday of the year and people had sprung up in their straw hats like mushrooms after rain. Those who knew Marthe did not dare to greet her; but she, not seeing that anything was amiss, said good afternoon to them quite unaffectedly. They must have regarded this as a gross piece of impertinence. She asked me how I had managed to leave the house. She laughed, then her face clouded over and, squeezing my fingers as tightly as she could, she thanked me for the risks I had taken. We walked back past her flat to deposit the basket. Actually I had thought up a fitting end to the adventures of this basket: wrapping up its contents and sending them off as a food-parcel for the Forces. But the idea was so shocking that I kept it to myself.

Marthe wanted to follow the Marne as far as La Varenne. We would have dinner opposite the Ile d'Amour. I said I would show her the Musée de l'Écu de France; it was the first museum I had ever seen and it had left a deep impression on me when I had been taken there as a child. I talked about it as if it was a place of exceptional interest. But when we saw that this museum was nothing but a joke, I did not want to admit that I had been taken in by it. Fulbert's scissors, indeed! I had believed it all. So I pretended that I had been playing a little trick on Marthe. She was rather puzzled by the whole business, since I was not in the habit of playing tricks. In fact, this disillusioning visit saddened me. 'Perhaps,' I said to myself, 'my love for Marthe will one day seem as much a deception as the Musée de I'Écu de France.'

For I often doubted the sincerity of her love. I sometimes wondered whether for her I was not a mere pastime – a caprice that she might abandon quite suddenly as peace-time recalled her to her conjugal duties. 'Yet,' I told myself, 'there are moments when lips and eyes cannot lie.' This is true, but there are also mean men who, when drunk, get angry if one refuses to accept their watch or their wallet. They are as sincere then as in their normal state. The times when one cannot lie are precisely those when one lies the most, above all to oneself. To believe a woman 'at a time when she cannot lie' is to believe in the sudden generosity of a miser.

My clear-sightedness was merely a more dangerous form of my naivety. In thinking that I was less naive, I was merely being naive in a different way, since one is naive at every age. And the naivety of old age is not the least of them. What I thought was my clear-sightedness threw a veil of gloom over everything and made me doubt Marthe's sincerity. Or rather, I began to doubt myself, thinking that I was not worthy of her. But if I had had a thousand times more proof of her love, I should not have been less unhappy.

I was too conscious of the value of what one never says to those one loves, for fear of seeming childish, not to feel profoundly disturbed by her reticence. It pained me that I was unable to penetrate her real thoughts.

I got home at half-past nine in the evening. My parents asked me about the walk. I described with great enthusiasm the forest of Sénart with its ferns that were twice as tall as a man. I talked of the charming village of Brunoy where we had had lunch. Suddenly, with an ironical smile, my mother interrupted me:

'Oh, by the way, René came round this afternoon. He was very surprised to learn that he had gone for a long walk with you.'

I was red with fury. This adventure, and many others, taught me that, despite a certain propensity for it, I will never make a good liar. I am always caught out. My parents said nothing more. They had had their modest triumph.

Twelve

In fact, my father was an unconscious accomplice of my first love affair. He even encouraged it, delighted that my precocity should find expression. He had always been afraid that I would fall into the clutches of a woman of ill repute. He was pleased that I had won the heart of a decent girl. He only began to disapprove when he learnt that Marthe wanted a divorce.

My mother, on the other hand, did not view our affair so benevolently. She was jealous. She regarded Marthe as a rival in my affections. She did not like Marthe, and failed to realize that she would have thought the same of any woman I happened to love. Moreover, she was much more concerned than my father with the what-will-people-say side of things. She was astonished that Marthe could compromise herself with a boy of my age. But then she had been brought up at F. And in all those small suburban communities beyond the working-class areas, one meets the same reactions and the same love of gossip that one finds in the provinces. Except that the proximity of Paris lends a greater sophistication to the gossip. Everybody must know his place. Thus because I had a mistress whose husband was at the Front, I gradually lost all my friends, under pressure from their parents. They disappeared in hierarchical order: from the notary's son to the son of our own gardener. My mother was deeply affected by these reactions – which I regarded as homage. She thought I was ruining my life for a woman who had gone out of her mind. She certainly blamed my father for having introduced her to me, and for turning a blind eye to subsequent events. But she considered that it was up to him to take the decisions, and as he did nothing she kept silent.

Thirteen

I spent every night at Marthe's. I arrived at half-past ten and left at five or six in the morning. I no longer jumped over the wall. I simply used my own key; but this openness required a certain amount of care. To prevent the bell ringing when I opened the gate, I wrapped some wadding round the clapper as I went out and took it off again the next morning when I came home.

No one in the house suspected my movements; the same could not be said of the people at J. For some time now the landlord and his wife and the old couple who lived downstairs had not troubled to conceal their disapproval of me, and they scarcely replied when I greeted them.

Each morning at five o'clock I would come down the stairs with my shoes in my hand in order to make as little noise as possible, and put them on again at the bottom. One morning I met the milk-boy on the stairs. He was carrying his milk-cans and I my shoes. He said good morning and grinned broadly. Marthe was lost. He was sure to go and tell the whole of J. what he had seen. But what caused me most discomfort was the fact that I looked so ridiculous. I could no doubt have bribed the boy to keep quiet but I didn't know how to set about it.

In the afternoon I dared not mention the episode to Marthe. In fact it could hardly make her position much worse: she was compromised already, and had been for a long time. Rumour had it that she was my mistress long before she was in reality. But we were quite unaware of this. However, we were soon to know the truth. One day I found Marthe in a particularly distraught state. The landlord had just informed her that for the last four days he had seen me leave at dawn. At first, he could hardly believe his eyes but there was no doubt about it. The old couple whose room was beneath Marthe's had complained of the noise we made night and day. Marthe was utterly crushed by the announcement and wanted to leave. It was no longer a question of taking more care to conceal our meetings. There was nothing more we could do: the trick had been taken. Marthe began to understand a number of things that had previously surprised her. The one friend she was really fond of, a Swedish girl, had stopped answering her letters. I discovered that the father of the family with whom she was staying had seen us one day arm-in-arm in the train and had advised the girl not to see Marthe again.

I made Marthe promise that if a row did break out, in any quarter, either with her parents or with her husband, she would stand firm. The threats of the landlord and the rumours that were rife made me both fear and hope that Marthe and Jacques would have to discuss their situation openly.

Marthe begged me to come and see her often while Jacques was on leave – she had already written to him about me. I refused; I was too afraid of playing my role badly when confronted with the sight of Marthe receiving the attentions of another man. His leave was eleven days. But what if he managed somehow to get another two days? I made Marthe swear that she would write to me every day. I waited for three days before going to the post office so as to be sure there would be a letter. There were four already. But I couldn't take them: I was short of one of my identity papers. I felt even less sure of myself because I had already altered the date on my birth-certificate – one had to be eighteen before one was eligible to use the *poste restante* service. I stood and argued with the woman behind the counter. I would have liked to throw pepper in her face and run off with the letters that she was holding in her hand but would not give me. At last, because they knew me at the post office they agreed to send the letters to me at home the next day.

I obviously had a long way to go to become a man. As I opened the first letter I wondered how she would tackle what seemed to me an extraordinarily difficult task: the writing of a love letter. I did not realize that it was the easiest kind of letter to write: all that was needed was love. I thought her letters were quite admirable, and worthy of the best that I had read. Yet she wrote only of quite ordinary things – and of the pain of separation.

I was surprised to find that I was not as violently jealous as I had expected. I was beginning to think of Jacques as 'the husband'. I gradually forgot how young he was, and pictured him as an old fogey.

I did not write to Marthe: it would have been altogether too risky. In fact, I was rather relieved that I did not have to write, feeling, as I did before anything new, a vague fear of inadequacy. I felt that my letters might have shocked her, or seemed naive.

After two days I was negligent enough to leave one of Marthe's letters lying on my desk. It disappeared; the next day, it was back on my desk. The discovery of this letter upset my plans. I had taken advantage of Jacques' leave – and the consequent amount of time I spent at home – to make my parents think that my feelings for Marthe had changed. For although at first I had almost gone out of my way to show my parents that I had a mistress I now began to wish that they had rather less proof. And now my father had learnt the real reason for my good behaviour.

I made use of this leisure to go back to my art classes; for some time now I had been using Marthe as the model for my nude drawings. I don't know whether my father had guessed this, but he did remark rather slyly once – and I couldn't help blushing – on the monotony of the models. So I went back to the Grande-Chaumière and worked hard, to provide myself with a supply of sketches that would last me for the rest of the year and which I would renew during the husband's next visit.

I also saw René again. He was now at the Lycée Louis-le-Grand. I met him every evening after my class at the Grande-Chaumière. We met in secret; since he had been expelled from Henri. IV, and above all since my affair with Marthe, his parents, who had formerly regarded me as a good influence, had forbidden him to see me.

René, who believed that love was an encumbrance in the pursuit of women, teased me about my passion for Marthe. I found that I could not bear his jibes and was cowardly enough to say that I did not really love Marthe. His admiration for me, which had recently been on the decline, immediately began to revive.

I began to take Marthe's love for granted. What tormented me most of all was the fast inflicted on my senses. My nerves were like those of a pianist without a piano, or a smoker without cigarettes.

René, who made fun of my love for Marthe, had nevertheless become attached to a woman, though he thought he did not love her. This graceful animal – a fair-haired Spanish girl – moved with such extraordinary suppleness that she might have belonged to a circus. Although René professed unconcern he was in fact extremely jealous. With a look compounded of both amusement and apprehension, he asked me to perform a strange service for him. This service – as anyone who knows schoolboys will realize – was of a typical schoolboy kind. He wanted to know if this woman would be unfaithful to him. My job was to make advances to her in order to find out.

I was very embarrassed by the whole affair. I felt my shyness getting the upper hand. Yet shyness was the very thing I wanted to conceal. However, the woman in question took the situation right out of my hands. She made such prompt advances to me that my shyness – and shyness, though it prevents one from doing certain things, forces one to do others – made me unable to fulfil my obligations to René and to Marthe. I hoped at least to find the experience pleasurable, but I was like a smoker who can only smoke one brand of cigarettes. So I was left only with remorse at having betrayed René. I swore to him that his mistress had spurned all my advances.

I felt no remorse in respect of Marthe though I certainly tried to. I told myself that I would never forgive her if she was unfaithful to me, but it was no use. 'It's not the same,' I said in excuse, with the remarkable vapidity that characterizes all egotism. Similarly I thought it quite natural not to write to Marthe, but if she had failed to write to me I would have taken it as an indication that she no longer loved me. However, this small infidelity on my part strengthened my love for her.

Fourteen

Jacques could not understand his wife's attitude towards him. Marthe, usually so talkative, did not say a word to him. If he asked her what was the matter, she replied: 'Nothing.'

Poor Jacques had trouble of a different kind with Mme Grangier. She accused him of treating her daughter too roughly and said she was sorry she had ever allowed her to marry him. She attributed to this rough treatment the sudden change that had come over her daughter. She decided that she wanted Marthe to go back and live with her. Jacques agreed. A few days after his arrival he accompanied Marthe to her mother's. Mme Grangier pandered to her daughter's slightest whims and thus, without knowing it, encouraged her in her love for me. Marthe had been born in that house. Everything there reminded her, she told Jacques, of the happy times she had spent there. She would sleep in the room she had slept in as a girl. Jacques thought that the least they might do was set up a bed for him in the same room. Marthe became hysterical. She would never allow the purity of that room to be sullied by his presence.

M. Grangier considered these scruples to be quite absurd. Mme Grangier retorted that neither he nor his son-in-law had any understanding of feminine sensibilities. She felt flattered that her daughter's heart should belong so little to Jacques. For Mme Grangier attributed to herself all the affection that Marthe refused her husband, and thought that her daughter's scruples were of the loftiest kind. They were indeed, but they were all on my account.

On the days when Marthe claimed to be most upset she insisted on going out. Jacques knew only too well that his company would not be appreciated on these walks. Marthe could not trust anyone with her letters to me, so she posted them herself.

I was all the more grateful for my enforced silence since, if I had been able to reply to her accounts of the tortures she was inflicting, it would have been to intercede for the victim. I was sometimes overcome with horror at the suffering I was causing; at other times I told myself that Marthe could never punish Jacques enough for the crime of having taken her virginity from me. But as nothing makes us less sentimental than passion, I was really only too pleased that I could not write and that Marthe should continue to drive Jacques to despair.

He left utterly downcast.

Marthe's hysterical behaviour was ascribed to the solitude in which she had been forced to live since her marriage. For her parents and husband were the only people who did not know of our affair; Marthe's landlord dared not say anything to Jacques out of respect for his uniform. Mme Grangier was already congratulating herself on having her daughter at home once more, as she had been before her marriage. So the Grangiers were all the more astonished when, the day after Jacques' departure, Marthe announced that she was going back to J.

I saw her again the same day. At first I scolded her gently for having been so hard on Jacques. But when I read Jacques' first letter I was panic-stricken. He said how easy it would be for him, if Marthe no longer loved him, to get himself killed.

I did not realize that this was simply a kind of blackmail. I saw myself as being responsible for someone's death, forgetting that this was precisely what I had wanted. My attitude became even more incomprehensible and unjust. Whichever way we turned, a wound was opened. Marthe tried hard to persuade me that it was kinder not to encourage Jacques' hopes, but I made her reply to the letter more gently than she wished. It was I who dictated the only tender letters he ever received from her. She wrote them against her will, in tears, as I threatened that I would never see her again if she disobeyed. That Jacques should owe his only happiness to me did something to mitigate my remorse.

I saw how superficial was his desire for suicide from the hope that filled the letters he wrote in reply to *ours*.

I was pleased with my attitude towards poor Jacques, though in fact it was motivated by egotism and by the fear of having a crime on my conscience.

Fifteen

These dramatic events were followed by a happier period. But because of my youth, and my weakness of character, a feeling of uncertainty still persisted. I lacked the necessary will-power either to desert Marthe – who might learn to forget me, and return to the path of duty – or to drive Jacques to his death. Our union was therefore at the mercy of the armistice, and the final return of the troops. If Jacques rejected his wife, she would be mine. If he finally decided to keep her, I felt incapable of taking her from him by force. Our happiness was a sand-castle. But the tide had no fixed time, and I hoped it would come in as late as possible.

Jacques was now utterly under Marthe's spell and it was he who defended her against her mother's anger at the return to J. Moreover, this return, aided by her own outraged feelings, had begun to arouse Mme Grangier's suspicions. There was something else, too, that struck her as being suspicious: Marthe refused to employ any servants, at which her family, and even more so her husband's family, were scandalized. But what could parents and parents-in-law do against Jacques, now that, as a result of the things I said to him through Marthe's letters, he had become our ally?

But suddenly J. opened fire on her.

The landlord and his wife no longer spoke to her. No one greeted her in the street. Only the tradesmen, for professional reasons, were more communicative. So Marthe, feeling a need sometimes for conversation, spent a more than usual amount of time in the shops. Sometimes, while I was there, she would go out to buy some milk and cakes. If she was not back within five minutes, I began to imagine she had been run over by a tram. I would run out to the dairy or the cake-shop and find her chatting there. I was furious at allowing myself to be so carried away by anxiety and as soon as we were outside the shop I accused her of having vulgar tastes and enjoying the conversation of tradesmen. Needless to say, the tradesmen, whose disquisitions I thus interrupted, hated me.

Court etiquette, like everything noble, is simple enough. But nothing is so enigmatic as the protocol of tradesmen. With them, the obsession with precedence is based primarily on age. Nothing would shock them more than an old duchess curtseying to a young prince. So one can imagine the feelings of a pastry cook or a dairyman's wife at having a mere boy come and interrupt their conversation with Marthe. But because of these conversations they forgave Marthe almost everything.

The landlord had a twenty-two-year-old son. When he came home on leave Marthe asked him to have tea with her.

That evening we heard angry voices from the floor below: the young man was forbidden to see the lodger again. I was so used to my father allowing me to do whatever I chose that I was quite astonished that the coward should take any notice of such an order.

The next day, as we were going out, he was digging in the garden. He was no doubt doing it as a punishment. In any case he was obviously embarrassed at seeing us and turned away so as to avoid having to say good afternoon.

These skirmishes hurt Marthe; she was intelligent enough and in love enough to realize that happiness is not to be found in the opinion of neighbours, but she was like those poets who, knowing that true poetry lies under a 'curse', nonetheless suffer because they cannot win the approbation they despise.

Sixteen

Local councillors seem always to play a part in my adventures. M. Marin, who lived on the floor below Marthe, a tall, upright old man with a grey beard, was a former councillor of J. Although he had given up his civic functions before the outbreak of war, he still liked to serve his country when the opportunity presented itself. He disapproved of the policies being pursued in the locality and lived quietly with his wife, visiting and entertaining only at the New Year.

For several days there had been a great deal of coming and going on the floor below. We could hear, from our room, every sound made even on the ground floor, so we knew exactly what was happening. The floor-polishers arrived. The maid, assisted by the landlord's maid, cleaned the silver in the garden and removed the verdigris from the brass lamps. We learned from the dairyman's wife that the Marins were going to give a party, but that the reason for it was being kept a secret. Mme Marin had invited the Mayor and begged him to allow her eight litres of milk. Would he also give the dairyman permission to make cream?

Permission was granted and on the day (a Friday) about fifteen local worthies arrived at the appointed time, accompanied by their wives. Each of these women had founded a society – for the propagation of maternal breast-feeding, or for aid to wounded soldiers, or some such cause – of which she was the president and the others members. The hostess, to gild the occasion, received her guests outside her front door. She had taken advantage of the secret attraction to turn her party into a sort of picnic. Each of her friends was to bring a dessert. All these women preached economy and were great inventors of recipes. Their creations were thus things like cakes without flour, creams made with lichen, etc. As each of them arrived she said to Mme Marin: 'It doesn't look very appetizing, but I think it will taste all right.'

M. Marin's interest in the party was to pave the way for his 'political comeback'.

Now the great 'surprise' was nothing less than Marthe and myself. A young man I often travelled with on the train, the son of one of the local worthies, had been indiscreet – and charitable – enough to inform me. Imagine my amazement when I learnt that one of the Marins' favourite entertainments was to stand under our bedroom in the late afternoon and listen to our love-making!

Perhaps they had acquired a real taste for it and wanted to share their pleasure with others. Of course, being respectable people, they explained their interest as a concern for morality. They wanted to share their revulsion with the most respected figures in the local community.

The guests were all seated. Mme Marin knew that I was with Marthe and had placed the table just under our bed. She was bursting with excitement. The entertainment was about to commence. But thanks to the young man, who had betrayed the secret partly to mystify his parents and partly out of solidarity with his own generation, we kept absolutely quiet. I had not dared to tell Marthe the real reason for the party. I thought of Mme Marin's drooping expression as the hands of the clock moved on, and of the impatience of her guests. At last, at about seven o'clock, the couples left, disappointed, muttering to each other that the Marins were imposters and calling poor M. Marin, who was at least seventy, a careerist. This would-be councillor promises the moon and cannot even wait to be elected before breaking his promises. As for Mme Marin, the local wives concluded that the party had simply been a means of providing herself with free desserts. The Mayor himself had stayed for only a few minutes; but these few minutes and the eight litres of milk inspired a rumour that he was on the very best of terms with the Marins' daughter, who was a schoolmistress. Mlle Marin had caused a scandal some years before by marrying a policeman – a position that was regarded as being unworthy of a schoolmistress's husband.

I punished the Marins still further by making them hear at last what they had hoped the others would hear. Marthe was surprised by my belated ardour. So, unable to keep it to myself any longer, and at the risk of causing her distress, I told her what had been the reason for the party. We laughed until the tears rolled down our cheeks.

Mme Marin, who might have proved more indulgent if I had fulfilled her hopes, did not forgive us for the disaster we had caused her. Her disapproval turned into hate. But she had no further means at her disposal to satisfy it, and she dared not resort to anonymous letters.

Seventeen

It was now May. I began to visit Marthe less frequently, and only slept there if I could tell a good enough lie at home to enable me to stay all night. I did this once or twice a week and was surprised that my lies never failed to be successful. In fact, my father did not believe them. He was so extraordinarily indulgent towards me that he closed his eyes to my activities, on condition only that my brothers and the servants remain in ignorance. So all I had to do was to say that I would be leaving the house at five o'clock in the morning, as on the day of my walk in the forest of Sénart. But my mother did not make up any more picnic baskets.

My father would agree to everything and then, suddenly putting his foot down, would scold me for not working. These sudden bursts of anger subsided as suddenly as they arose, like waves.

Nothing is so absorbing as love. One is not really lazy because, being in love, one has quite naturally no time for anything else. Love feels, rather obscurely, that its only possible distraction lies in work. So it regards work as a rival – and love can brook no rival. But love is a beneficent form of laziness, like the soft rain that fertilizes the ground on which it falls.

If youth is foolish, it is because young people are not allowed to be lazy. The great fault of our educational system is that, because of the numbers involved, it is designed for the mediocre child. For a lively mind there is no such thing as laziness. I never learned more than during these long days when, to an outside observer, I would have appeared to be wasting my time. In fact, I was studying my heart's apprenticeship as a social climber studies his table-manners.

When I did not sleep at Marthe's, that is to say most days, we went down to the Marne after dinner and stayed out until eleven o'clock. I untied my father's rowing-boat. Marthe took the oars, while I lay down with my head on her lap. I would get in her way and suddenly a blow from one of the oars would remind me that our outing would not last for ever.

Love wishes to share its happiness. A woman who is cool by nature becomes demonstrative, kisses you in the nape of the neck and invents innumerable tricks to distract you if you happen to be writing a letter. I never wanted to kiss Marthe so much as when her attention was taken up by something else; or to touch her hair and undo it as when she was pinning it up. In the boat I would throw myself upon her and smother her with kisses to make her let go of the oars and let the boat lose its way among the herbs and the white and yellow water-lilies. She saw this as a sign of uncontrollable passion, whereas I was really in the grip of this powerful urge to disturb her. We would then moor the boat behind some tall tufts of grass. The danger of being seen or of capsizing the boat made our sport all the more pleasurable.

Nor did I complain of the hostility of the landlord and his wife who made my presence in Marthe's rooms so difficult.

My obsessive desire to possess Marthe as Jacques had never been able to, to kiss some part of her skin after making her swear that no other lips but mine had touched it, was really only a kind of profligacy. But did I admit it? All love has a youth, a maturity and an old age. Was I already at that final stage when love no longer satisfied me unless accompanied each time by some new trick? For if my pleasure was based on habit, it thrived on the thousand and one slight changes it imposed on habit. It is not primarily by increasing the doses, which would soon become lethal, that an addict finds ecstasy, but in the rhythm he invents, either by changing the times, or by employing various deceptions to confuse the organism.

I loved that left bank of the Marne so much that I used to cross over on to the other side, which was so very different, in order to contemplate the side I loved. The right bank is more harsh. It is occupied by farmers and market-gardeners, whereas mine is left to idlers. We moored the boat to a tree and went and lay in the corn. The field shivered in the evening breeze. Our selfish desire succeeded in forgetting prejudice, sacrificing the corn to the comfort of our love as it had sacrificed Jacques.

Eighteen

The scent of uncertainty sharpened my senses. Because I had tasted other, more violent pleasures, more like those one experiences unlovingly with a chance encounter, my taste for simpler pleasures had been dulled.

I was already beginning to appreciate the freedom of chaste sleep, the feeling of well-being at lying alone between fresh sheets. I pleaded reasons of prudence to avoid spending the night with Marthe. She admired my strength of character. I also wished to avoid the irritation aroused in me by the angelic tone of voice that women – they are all natural actresses – adopt on waking and which gives the impression that they emerge each morning from the Beyond.

I reproached myself for my criticisms and my deceptions and spent whole days wondering whether I loved Marthe more or less than before. My love made everything seem more complicated. I misinterpreted everything Marthe said, forever seeking a deeper meaning in her words; I misinterpreted her silences, too. Was I always so wrong? A certain shock, impossible to describe, warns us when we come near to the truth. My pleasures – and also my anxieties – became stronger. The sudden desire that would come over me, as I lay beside her, to be alone in my own bed at home gave me a glimpse of how unbearable living together would be. On the other hand, I could not imagine living without Marthe. I was beginning to experience the punishments of adultery.

I now held it against Marthe that she had agreed, before we became lovers, to furnish Jacques' home according to my wishes. The furniture, which I had chosen not for my own pleasure, but to displease Jacques, now became hateful to me. For no apparent reason, I had grown tired of it. I regretted that I had not allowed Marthe to choose her own furniture. I might not have liked it at first, but there would have been the pleasure, later, of coming round to it out of love for her. I was jealous that it was Jacques who would now enjoy that pleasure.

Marthe stared at me wide-eyed when I told her bitterly: 'I hope you won't keep this furniture when we live together.' She respected whatever I said. Thinking that I had forgotten that it was I who had chosen it, she dared not remind me of the fact, but secretly deplored my bad memory.

Nineteen

At the beginning of June Marthe got a letter from Jacques in which, for once, he spoke of other things than of his love for her. He was ill. He was to be evacuated to the hospital at Bourges. I derived no pleasure from learning that he was ill, but I was relieved that at last he had something to say. The following day or the day after that he would be passing through J. and he begged Marthe to be on the platform and watch for the train. Marthe showed me the letter. She expected an order from me.

Love had turned her into a slave. Confronted by her unconditional obedience I found it hard to give an order either one way or the other. In my eyes, my silence meant that I consented. Could I stop her seeing her husband for the space of a few seconds? She too was silent. So, by a kind of tacit agreement, I did not go and see her the next day.

The day after that, in the morning, a messenger-boy arrived at my parents' with a note which he handed to me personally as he had been instructed. It was from Marthe. She was waiting for me down by the river. She begged me to come if I still felt any love for her.

I ran all the way to the seat where Marthe was waiting for me. Her greeting, so little in keeping with the style of her note, chilled my heart. I thought she no longer loved me.

What had happened was that Marthe had taken my silence of two days before as a mark of hostility. It had never crossed her mind that there was any tacit agreement between us. Now her hours of anguish were followed by the pain of seeing me alive, for nothing less than death should have prevented my coming the day before. My amazement was quite unfeigned. I explained my feeling of respect for her duties towards her sick husband. She only half believed me. This annoyed me. I nearly blurted out: 'When for once I don't lie . . .' We both burst into tears.

But these confused games of chess can be interminable and exhausting if one of the players does not bring a little order into things. Marthe's attitude to Jacques was hardly flattering. I took her in my arms and kissed her. 'Silence doesn't suit us,' I said. We promised never to conceal from each other even our most secret thoughts. I felt a little sorry for her that she should believe such a thing to be possible.

At J. Jacques had looked in vain for Marthe. Then, as the train passed in front of their house, he had seen that the shutters were open. He wrote begging her to reassure him. He asked her to come to Bourges. 'You must go,' I said, in such a way that this simple sentence might not be interpreted as a reproach.

'All right, I'll go,' she said, 'if you come with me.'

This was carrying innocence a little far. But the love that was expressed even in her most shocking words or actions led me rapidly from anger to gratitude. I reacted violently at first, then controlled myself. I spoke to her gently. Her naivety moved me. I treated her like a child that asks for the moon.

I tried to explain how immoral it would be for her to be accompanied by me. The fact that my reply was not, like that of an outraged lover, spoken in anger, gave it greater weight. It was the first time she had heard me use the word 'moral'. It could not have had a more happy effect. Like me, she too must occasionally have had doubts as to the morality of our love. Had I never used that word she might have thought I was amoral, for, despite her revolt against the excellent bourgeois prejudices, she remained profoundly bourgeois. But now that I had, for the first time, appealed to her conscience, it was clear that I regarded everything that we had done up till then as perfectly legitimate.

Marthe was sorry to miss this outrageous 'honeymoon'. She now realized how impossible it would have been.

'At least,' she said, 'allow me not to go.'

This word 'moral', spoken almost in passing, made me her spiritual director. I used this position as a despot uses some new-found power. Power draws attention to itself only when used unjustly. So I replied that I could see nothing wrong in her not going to Bourges. I found her good enough reasons to convince her of this: the journey would be very tiring for her and, anyway, Jacques would soon come home to convalesce. These reasons were found valid enough by her parents-in-law, if not by Jacques.

By turning Marthe in whatever direction happened to suit me I was gradually remaking her in my own image. I blamed myself for doing this, and for knowingly destroying our happiness. That she should begin to resemble me, to become my creation, both delighted and angered me. I saw it as a reason for our compatibility. But I also saw it as a cause of disasters to come. In fact, I had gradually communicated to her my uncertainty – an uncertainty which, when the day for decisions came, would prevent her from taking any. I saw how her weakness was like my own; we hoped that the sea would spare our sand-castle, whereas other children hasten to build higher up the shore.

Very often such a spiritual resemblance finds expression on the physical plane, in an expression of the eyes or in the way one walks. On several occasions, strangers took us for brother and sister. There must exist within us seeds of resemblance that are germinated by love. Even the most prudent lovers sooner or later give themselves away by a gesture or an inflexion of the voice.

It must be admitted that if the heart has its reasons which

reason knows nothing of, it is because the reason is less reasonable than the heart. No doubt we are all like Narcissus, loving and hating our own reflection, but indifferent to all others. It is this instinct for resemblance that leads us through life; it is this that makes us pause to admire a certain landscape, a certain woman, a particular poem. We can admire others without feeling this shock. The instinct for resemblance is the only rule of conduct that is not artificial. But in society only the grosser spirits appear not to contravene the rules of morality, always remaining loyal to the same type. Some men, for example, go blindly for 'blondes', unaware that the deepest resemblances are often the most secret.

Twenty

For several days Marthe had seemed unusually preoccupied, though not in a sad way. If she had also been sad I could have explained her preoccupation by the approach of 15 July, the date she would be joining Jacques' family and the convalescent Jacques at a resort on the Channel coast. It was now Marthe's turn to be silent; she jumped at the sound of my voice. She bore with the unbearable: visits to her family, snubs from neighbours, bitter, suggestive remarks from her mother and the bluff teasing of her father, who presumed she had a lover without really believing it.

Why did she put up with it all? Was it because I had so often reproached her with attaching too much importance to things that did not matter? She seemed happy, but happy in an odd, almost embarrassed way, which I found disagreeable, since I did not share it. I, who had criticized her childishness in interpreting my silence as indifference, now accused her of no longer loving me because she talked less.

Marthe dared not tell me that she was pregnant.

Twenty-one

I should have liked to have appeared pleased at hearing the news. But at first I was quite stunned. Having never dreamt that I could be responsible for anything whatsoever, I found that I was responsible for something of the utmost gravity. I was also angry with myself for not being man enough to treat the whole thing as a simple matter. Marthe had only spoken under pressure. She was afraid that instead of bringing us closer together, the news might separate us. I simulated cheerfulness so well that she lost all her fears. She was so deeply imbued with bourgeois morality that for her this child was a sign that God approved of our love, and did not see it as a crime meriting punishment.

Whereas Marthe regarded her pregnancy as a reason why I should never leave her, it filled me with consternation. It seemed to me impossibly unjust that our youth should be shackled in this way. For the first time I began to have worries of a material kind: we could be cut off by our families.

I loved this child already and it was because I loved it that I rejected it. I had no wish to be responsible for the troubled life it would have. I could not have lived such a life myself.

Instinct is our guide; a guide that leads us to perdition. Yesterday Marthe had feared that her pregnancy would drive us apart. Today, loving me more than ever, she thought that my love was growing like her own. Yesterday I had rejected this unborn child; today I began to love it and in doing so lost some of my love for

Marthe, just as at the beginning of our affair my heart had given her what it withdrew from others.

As I put my lips to Marthe's belly it was not she I was kissing, it was my own child. Marthe, alas, was no longer my mistress, but a mother.

Never again did I feel that we were alone together. There was always this witness, to whom we were responsible for everything we did. I found it hard to accept this sudden change, which I blamed entirely on Marthe; and yet I felt that I would have forgiven her even less if she had lied to me. At certain moments I felt that her son was not mine and that Marthe might be lying in order to perpetuate our love.

Like a sick man seeking ease, I did not know which way to turn. I felt that I no longer loved the same Marthe and that my son would only be happy if he believed Jacques to be his father. The implications of this were disturbing, of course. I would have to leave Marthe. On the other hand it was no use priding myself on my manhood; the present situation was too serious for me to believe in the feasibility of such an unreasonable (by which I meant 'reasonable') course.

Twenty-two

For Jacques would come home in the end. After this strange interlude he would find, like so many soldiers betrayed because of the exceptional nature of the circumstances, a sad, docile wife, of whose misconduct there would be no sign. But the child could only be accounted for to her husband if she agreed to have intercourse with him during the holiday. I was cowardly enough to urge her to do so.

But of all our disagreements this was far from being the strangest or the most painful. Indeed, I was surprised to encounter so little opposition. It was only later that I learnt the reason for this. Marthe had not dared to tell me that, in fact, she had given in to Jacques the last time he was home on leave and was hoping – while pretending to obey me – to plead her pregnancy as a reason for rejecting him during their holidays at Granville. The whole business was further complicated by a series of dates, the improbability of which would leave no one in any doubt when the time came for Marthe's confinement. 'There's time yet,' I told myself. 'Marthe's parents will be afraid of a scandal. They'll take her to the country to have the child, and they'll delay the announcement.'

The date of Marthe's departure was approaching. I could only benefit from her absence. It would be a sort of trial. I hoped I would be able to cure myself of my love for her. If I failed – if my love proved too green to be plucked off – I knew that when Marthe returned I would find her as faithful as myself.

She left on 12 July, at seven in the morning. I spent the night before with her at J. I had promised myself beforehand that I would not spend one minute of the night asleep. I would lay up such a store of caresses as would last me for the rest of my days.

A quarter of an hour after going to bed I fell asleep.

Usually Marthe's presence disturbed my sleep. For the first time I slept as well beside her as I did alone.

When I woke, she was already up. She had not dared to wake me. In half-an-hour she would be catching the train into Paris. I was furious with myself for wasting the last few precious hours we had together. She was crying too, at having to go. I would have preferred us to spend our last few minutes doing something other than kissing away our tears.

Marthe left me her key and asked me to go there often to think about us and to write my letters to her at her table.

I had sworn that I would not accompany her to Paris. But I could not repress my desire for her lips and, as I was craven enough to want to love her less, I attributed this desire to the fact that she was leaving, that this was the 'last time'. I knew perfectly well, of course, that there would be no 'last time' unless she wanted it.

At the Gare Montparnasse, where she was meeting her parents-in-law, I kissed her quite openly. Again my excuse was that, if her parents-in-law were suddenly to appear, the ensuing scene would at least bring the whole matter to a head.

Back at F., where I was used to spending my time waiting for my next visit to Marthe, I tried to keep myself occupied. I dug the garden. I tried to read. I played hide-and-seek with my sisters – a thing I had not done for five years. In the evenings, so as not to arouse suspicion, I had to go out for a walk as usual. Usually I hardly noticed the walk to the Marne. But that evening I kept twisting my foot on stones and it seemed endless. As I lay in the boat I wished, for the first time, that I was dead. But since I was as incapable of dying as I was of living I would have to depend on the services of some charitable assassin. I regretted that one can not die of boredom or anguish. Gradually my head emptied, with a sound like bath-water running out. One last, extended gurgle and my head was empty. I fell asleep.

I awoke in the cold of a July dawn. I went home, chilled to the bone. I found the house bustling with activity. I was met in the hall by my father, who did not conceal his disapproval. My mother was not well, and he had sent the housemaid to get me up so that I could go and fetch the doctor. So my absence was official.

Throughout the ensuing scene I could not but admire the instinctive delicacy with which this good judge chose, from hundreds of apparently blameworthy deeds, the very one of which I could justly plead innocence. But I did not do so; it would have been too difficult. I let my father think that I had been to J., and when he forbade me to go out after dinner I could not help feeling grateful to him for acting once again as my accomplice. He had supplied me with an excuse for not having to spend the time alone out of doors.

I sat around waiting for the postman. It was all I lived for. I was incapable of making any effort to forget her.

Marthe had given me a paper-knife that I was to use only to open her letters. But it was no use: I was too impatient. I tore open the letters as soon as I had them in my hands. Each time I felt ashamed and resolved to keep them unopened for a quarter of an hour. In this way I hoped in the end to regain control over myself and keep the letters in my pocket, unopened. But each time I had to postpone the inauguration of this system to the following day.

Once I was so angry with myself at my own weakness that I

tore up one of the letters without reading it. But I had no sooner thrown the pieces of paper about the garden than I was down on my knees picking them up again. The letter contained a photograph of Marthe. I was very superstitious, attributing a tragic significance to the most minor incidents. I had torn up a picture of her face. I saw this as a warning from heaven. I regained my calm only after spending four hours sticking the letter and the photograph together again. I had never worked so hard in my life. My fear that some misfortune might befall Marthe sustained me during this absurd task that exhausted my eyes and my nerves.

A specialist had recommended that Marthe go sea-bathing. While fully aware of how unjust I was being, I told her she was not to do so. I did not want anyone else to see her body.

And since Marthe was to spend a month at Granville in any case, I was actually pleased that Jacques would be with her. I remembered the photograph of herself in white that Marthe had shown me the day we chose her furniture. Nothing made me more apprehensive than the idea of other young men on the beach. I imagined them at once to be much more handsome, stronger and more self-assured than I.

Her husband would protect her against them.

At certain moments of great tenderness, feeling like a drunk who wants to embrace everyone in sight, I thought of writing to Jacques, telling him that I was Marthe's lover and asking him to take good care of her. Sometimes I envied Marthe for being adored by both Jacques and me. Should we not strive together to make her happy? In these moments of crisis I felt like a complaisant lover. I would have liked to become acquainted with Jacques, to explain things to him, to show him that we ought not to be jealous of each other. Then, suddenly, a wave of hatred would sweep away these fond day-dreams.

Twenty-three

In every letter Marthe asked me to go to her flat. Her persistence reminded me of one of my very devout aunts who was always reproaching me for never visiting my grandmother's grave. I have never liked pilgrimages; such boring duties demean the idea of death, of love.

Can one not think of a dead woman, or of one's absent mistress, elsewhere than in a cemetery or in a certain room? I did not try to explain this to Marthe and told her that I did go to her flat; just as I used to tell my aunt that I went to the cemetery. However, as it happens, I was to go to Marthe's – but in rather strange circumstances.

One day, on the train, I met the young Swedish girl who had been told by the family she was staying with not to see Marthe.

Perhaps because I was lonely, I found myself quite attracted to this girl's childish ways. I suggested that she should come to J. in secret and have tea with us the following day. Naturally, I did not tell her that Marthe would not be there, for fear of frightening her off. Indeed, I said how pleased Marthe would be to see her again. I swear that I did not really know what I expected to do. I was behaving like one of those children who have just made each other's acquaintance and are trying to astonish each other. I could not resist seeing the expression of surprise or anger on Svea's angelic face when I had to tell her that Marthe wasn't there.

Yes, I think it must have been just such a childish desire to astonish, because I could find very little of interest to say to her, while she, on the other hand, had a certain exotic quality, and surprised me with every sentence she spoke. Nothing is more delightful than the sudden intimacy that can spring up between people who hardly know each other. She wore round her neck a small, blue-enamelled, gold cross that hung over a rather ugly dress – which I redesigned to my own taste. She was like a live doll. I felt more and more strongly that I should like to continue our conversation somewhere other than in a railway carriage.

However, her convent-girl manner was spoilt by the fact that she looked like one of those girls who go to commercial college – and, indeed, she did go to just such a place, where she studied for an hour a day, without much benefit, French and typing. She showed me her typing exercises. Almost every letter was wrong and had been corrected in the margin by her teacher. From a frightful handbag, which she had obviously made herself, she took out a cigarette-case adorned with a coronet. She offered me a cigarette. She did not smoke herself but she always carried this cigarette-case because her friends smoked. She told me about Swedish customs that I pretended I had heard of: Midsummer Night, bilberry jam, and so on. She then took out of her handbag a photograph of her twin sister that she had received from Sweden only the day before – naked, on horseback, with their grandfather's top hat on her head. I blushed scarlet. Her sister was so like her that I thought at first that she was playing a trick on me and that the picture was of herself. I bit my lip to stop myself from kissing her. I must have looked pretty bestial, for she suddenly looked rather frightened and her eyes searched for the alarm-signal.

She arrived at Marthe's the following day at four o'clock. I told her that Marthe was in Paris, but would be back shortly. And I added: 'Marthe forbade me to let you go before she comes back.' I intended to own up to my plan only at the last minute.

Fortunately, she was hungry. My own hunger took a novel form. The tart and the raspberry ice-cream did not tempt me; what I wanted was to be the tart and the ice-cream that she brought to her lips. My own lips twisted into involuntary grimaces.

I wanted Svea not out of lust, but out of greed. If she had refused her lips, her cheeks would have satisfied me.

I spoke slowly, pronouncing each syllable carefully, to help her understand what I said. Stimulated by this entertaining tea-party, I became impatient at not being able to speak more quickly – though normally I was far from talkative. I felt a need for conversation and for childish confidences. I put my ear close to her mouth. I drank in every word she spoke.

I had made her drink a liqueur. Afterwards, I felt sorry for her: it was like making a little bird drunk. I hoped, nevertheless, that this would serve my purpose, for it did not matter to me whether she offered her lips willingly or not. I thought how unseemly it was that such a scene should take place in Marthe's own room. But I repeated to myself: 'It does not in any way detract from our love.' I wanted Svea as one wants a fruit – and no mistress could be jealous of a fruit.

I held her hand in my own clumsy hands. I would have liked to undress her and rock her to sleep. She lay down on the sofa. I raised myself and bent my lips to the fine down at the nape of her neck. I did not assume from her silence that my kisses had given her any pleasure; but she was incapable of indignation and could think of no polite way of rejecting me in French. I nibbled at her cheeks, fully expecting a sweet juice to squirt out, as from a peach.

At last I kissed her lips. My patient victim submitted to my caresses, her mouth and eyes closed. Her only gesture of refusal was to move her head feebly from left to right, and from right to left. I did not delude myself, but my mouth took this to be the response it desired. I felt with her as I had never felt with Marthe.

This resistance which was no resistance gratified both my boldness and my indolence. I was naive enough to imagine that things would continue in the same fashion and that I would succeed in raping her without difficulty.

I had never undressed a woman before; on the contrary they had always undressed me. As a result, my attempts to do so were clumsy in the extreme. I began by taking off her shoes and stockings. I kissed her feet and legs. But when I tried to undo her bodice, Svea fought like a tigress, for all the world as if she was a little girl who had refused to go to bed and had to be undressed by force. She kicked out at me wildly. I caught hold of her feet, held them tightly and smothered them with kisses. At last I reached the point of satiety, just as one's greed is blunted by too much cream and too many cakes. I had to admit my deceit and tell her that Marthe was away. I made her promise that if she ever saw Marthe again she would not tell her about our meeting. I did not admit openly that I was Marthe's lover, but I hinted that I was. It was this air of mystery that prompted her to reply, when I asked her out of politeness whether we would see each other again, that she would see me the following day.

I did not go back to Marthe's. And perhaps Svea did not, after all, go back and ring at the closed door. I was aware of how badly, according to conventional morality, I had behaved. For it had probably only been the circumstances of our meeting that had made Svea seem desirable. Would I really have wanted her anywhere else but in Marthe's room?

But I felt no remorse. I abandoned her not out of regard for Marthe, but because I had taken all the sweetness from her.

A few days later I received a letter from Marthe. Enclosed was a letter from her landlord saying that his house was not a brothel and that I had used the key to her rooms and entertained a woman there. Marthe added that she had proof of my infidelity and that she would never see me again. This would no doubt make her unhappy, but she would rather be unhappy than deceived.

I knew that these threats were quite harmless and that it needed only a lie – or even, if need be, the truth – to dispel them. But I was vexed that in writing to break off our relationship she did not mention suicide. I accused her of coldness. I considered that her letter did not merit an explanation. If I had been in a similar situation, I would have thought it only proper to threaten Marthe with suicide – without, of course, having the slightest intention of carrying out my threat. This was the schoolboy in me: I imagined that the code of love made certain lies obligatory.

A new task in my apprenticeship to love now presented itself: to exculpate myself in Marthe's eyes and to accuse her of having more confidence in her landlord than in me. I explained to her how clever this latest manoeuvre of the Marin camp was. Svea had in fact come to see her one day as I was writing in her room, and I had let her in because I had already seen her through the window and I knew that Marthe would not want her to think that she approved of people's attempts to keep them apart. She had probably come in secret and at great inconvenience to herself.

I added that I could assure Marthe that Svea's feelings towards her had in no way changed. And I ended by saying how comforting it had been to talk about Marthe, in her own room, to her closest friend.

This alarm made me curse the fact that love places us in the situation of having to justify our actions, when I would so much have liked never to have to justify anything I did, even to myself.

And yet, I told myself, love must offer a great many advantages, since all men entrust it with their freedom. I hoped I would soon be strong enough to do without love and so not have to sacrifice any of my desires. I did not yet know that when it comes to servitude, it is better to be enslaved by one's heart than the slave of one's passions.

Just as a bee plunders in order to enrich the hive, a lover enriches his love with every passing desire that besets him in the street. It is his mistress who benefits from this accumulation. I had not yet discovered this discipline that gives fidelity to unfaithful natures. When a man, lusting after a girl, transfers this ardour to the woman he loves, his desire is the stronger for being unsatisfied, and will lead the woman to believe that no one has ever loved her so much. It is a form of infidelity, though in most people's opinion morality has triumphed. Such duplicity leads to profligacy. One should not condemn too readily therefore men who are capable of infidelity at the very height of their love; they should not be accused of frivolity. They reject this easy subterfuge and refuse to confuse their happiness with their pleasure.

Marthe expected me to exculpate myself. She begged me to forgive her for her reproaches. I did so, but not without expressing a certain reluctance. Ironically she wrote to the landlord, asking him to allow me during her absence to entertain one of her friends.

Twenty-four

When Marthe returned at the end of August, she did not go back to her flat at J. but returned instead to her parents' house, the Grangiers themselves having decided to stay on at the coast. This new setting, in which Marthe had spent her whole life, acted as an aphrodisiac on me. Sexual fatigue and my unavowed desire to sleep alone disappeared. I never slept at home. I was aflame. I acted with all the haste of someone who is to die young and consumes life at the double. I wanted to have as much as I could of Marthe before motherhood spoiled her.

Our bedroom was the one in which Marthe had slept throughout her childhood, and which she had refused to allow Jacques to enter. When I looked up from her narrow bed my eyes met her First Communion picture. I made her stare at another photograph of herself, this time as a baby, so that our child would take after her. I wandered, enchanted, around the house where she had been born and where she had grown up. In a lumber-room I found her cradle – I wanted it to be used again – and I got her to show me the brassieres and knickers she had worn when she lived at home.

I had no regrets for the flat at J., where the furniture lacked the charm of the uglier family variety. It had nothing to teach me. But here, in this house, every small piece of furniture against which, perhaps, she had bumped her head as a little girl, spoke to me of Marthe. Then again, we were on our own, without any councillors or landlords to bother us. We disported ourselves as freely as savages, walking almost naked around the garden as if it were a desert island. We lay on the lawn and had afternoon tea beneath a tunnel of birthwort, honeysuckle and virginia creeper. Mouth to mouth, we fought over bursting plums that were still warm from the sun when I picked them up. My father had never been able to get me to look after the garden, as my brothers did, but I worked hard on Marthe's, raking and weeding. At the end of a hot day I felt the same heady masculine pride in quenching the thirst of the soil and the suppliant flowers as in satisfying a woman's desire. I had always regarded goodness as being rather foolish; but I now understood its real strength. The flowers bloomed because I had watered them and the hens slept quietly in the shade after I had thrown them their corn: how good! And how selfish! Dead flowers and scraggy hens would have brought an element of sadness into our island of love. The water and the corn were more for myself than for the flowers and the hens.

In this renewal of the heart I forgot or despised my recent discoveries. The profligacy provoked by this shrine of family life I saw as the end of my profligacy. That last week of August and the month of September were the only time in my life when I was really happy. I did not cheat or lie, nor was I wounding myself, nor did I wound Marthe. I could see no further obstacles before us. At sixteen I envisaged a mode of life such as one usually yearns for in maturity. We would live in the country and remain there for ever, eternally young.

Lying beside her on the lawn, stroking her face with a blade of grass, I explained to Marthe, slowly and carefully, what our life would be like. Since her return, Marthe had been looking for a flat for us in Paris. When I told her that I wanted to live in the country, she almost burst into tears. 'I'd never have dared to suggest that,' she said. 'I thought you'd get bored being alone with me all the time and that you needed to be in town.' 'How little you really know me,' I replied. I would have liked to live near Mandres, where we had gone walking one day and where they grow roses. Later, one evening when we had had dinner in Paris and caught the last train home, I smelled the roses in the station. Huge cases of them were being unloaded in the goods-yard and all around the air was heavy with their scent. Throughout my childhood I had heard people speak of this mysterious 'rose train' that passed at a time when children are in bed and asleep.

'But the roses aren't there all the year round,' said Marthe. 'Don't you think you might find Mandres a rather ugly place when the roses are finished? Wouldn't it be wiser to choose somewhere that's less beautiful, but not so changeable?'

This was very typical of me. The desire to feast my senses for two months on roses had made me forget the other ten – and the fact that I had wanted to live in Mandres provided me with yet another proof of the ephemeral nature of our love.

Offering as an excuse some excursion or invitation I often did not go home for dinner, but stayed with Marthe instead.

One afternoon I found her with a young man in Air Force uniform. It was her cousin. I was careful to greet her with all due formality, but Marthe got up and kissed me. Her cousin laughed at my embarrassment. 'We can say what we like in front of Paul, darling,' she said. 'I've told him everything.' I was embarrassed, but also delighted that Marthe should have told her cousin that she loved me. This charming but rather light-headed young man, whose only worry was that his uniform might not be in order, seemed to approve most heartily of our affair. He saw it as a fine trick played on Jacques, whom he despised for not being in the Air Force and for not frequenting bars.

Paul talked about all the games they had played in the garden when they were children. I questioned him endlessly, avid for any information that would show Marthe in a new, unexpected light. At the same time it made me sad. For I was too close to childhood to have forgotten the games that parents are quite unaware of, either because grown-ups retain no memory of them or because they regard them as a necessary evil. I was jealous of Marthe's past.

Our account of how much the landlord hated us and of the party at the Marins' put Paul in high good humour and he offered us the use of his flat in Paris.

I noticed that Marthe dared not tell him that we were planning to live together. I felt that he was in favour of our affair because it amused him, but that he would cry with the pack in the event of a scandal.

Marthe got up from the table and waited on us. The servants had gone with Mme Grangier to the sea-side, for Marthe had been prudent enough to insist that she preferred living like Robinson Crusoe. Her parents, thinking her an incorrigible romantic, and believing that romantics, like madmen, must not be contradicted, left her alone.

We stayed for a long time at table. Paul raided the cellar for the best bottles of wine. We were very gay – a gaiety we would no doubt regret, for Paul was behaving like the confidant of any common-or-garden adultery. He poked fun at Jacques. If I had kept quiet, I might have shown up his lack of tact. So I joined in the game, preferring that to humiliating this easy-going cousin.

When we saw the time, we realized that Paul had missed the last train back to Paris. Marthe offered him a bed for the night. He accepted. I gave Marthe such a look that she added at once: 'Of course, you'll stay too, darling.' When Paul said goodnight to us at our bedroom door and kissed his cousin on the cheek in the most natural way imaginable, I felt as if I was in my own house, that I was Marthe's husband and that a cousin of my wife's was staying with us.

Twenty-five

By the end of September I really felt that to say goodbye to that house would be the end of our happiness. After a few more months of grace we would have to choose either to live a lie or to admit the truth openly, neither of which would be particularly easy. Because it was so important that Marthe should not be abandoned by her parents before the birth of our child, I plucked up courage at last to ask Marthe whether her mother knew that she was pregnant. Marthe said that she did, and that she had also told Jacques. I then realized that she sometimes told me lies, since in May, after Jacques' leave, she had sworn to me that he had not touched her.

Twenty-six

The days were growing shorter and shorter; and the coolness of the night air put an end to our walks. It was difficult to meet at J. To avoid a scandal we had to be as cautious as thieves and wait in the street for the Marins and the landlord to go out.

The sadness of those October days, when the evenings were too cool to spend outside, yet not cold enough to light the fire, drove us to bed by about five o'clock. At home, such an early retirement meant only one thing: one was ill. So I was particularly amused by this five o'clock bedtime. I could not imagine that other people were doing the same. I was alone with Marthe, in bed, the still point of an active world. I hardly dared to look at Marthe's naked body. What sort of monster was I? I now began to feel remorse for the noblest act a man can perform. When I thought how I had spoiled Marthe's graceful beauty and saw how her belly was swelling, I regarded myself as nothing better than a vandal. When I used to bite her, at the beginning of our affair, she would say: 'Mark me!' Had I not marked her in the worst possible way?

Not only was Marthe the most loved – which is not to say the best loved – of mistresses, but she had driven everything else from my mind. I did not even think about my friends; on the contrary, I was afraid of them, knowing that they would consider themselves to be doing us a good turn if they succeeded in deflecting us from our chosen path. Fortunately, a man's friends cannot tolerate his mistresses and think them unworthy of him. This is his only safeguard. When it is no longer so, a man's mistress is well on the way to leaving him for one of his friends.

Twenty-seven

My father was beginning to get alarmed. But because he had always taken my side against his sister and my mother, he did not want to appear to be shifting ground. However, without a word to them about it, he had secretly come round to their position. When he talked to me, he said he would do anything to take me away from Marthe. He would inform her parents, her husband, etc. The next day he would do nothing to stop me going out.

I knew his weaknesses and exploited them. I answered him back. I attacked him with the same arguments that my mother and my aunt used against him. I reproached him with trying to exercise his authority when it was too late. Had it not been his wish that I should meet Marthe? He, in turn, piled reproaches on his own head. An atmosphere of tragedy reigned over the house. What an example I was for my two brothers! My father was clearly envisaging the day when they would justify their own ill conduct by mine.

Until then he had thought it was no more than an innocent infatuation. But, once again, my mother found some letters, in which Marthe spoke of our future and our child! Triumphantly, she presented her evidence to my father.

My mother still thought of me too much as a child to consider it reasonable that I should present her with a grandson or granddaughter. It seemed quite impossible that she could become a grandmother at her age. Indeed, for her this was the final proof that the child could not be mine.

It is strange how innocence can lead people to think the worst of others. My mother, with her profound innocence, could not admit that a woman could be unfaithful to her husband. For her, such an act was of so outrageous a nature that it could not be the result of love. If I was Marthe's lover, she must inevitably have other lovers as well. My father knew perfectly well that such reasoning was false, but he used it nonetheless to sow seeds of doubt in my mind. In this way he hoped to weaken my love for Marthe. He implied that I was the only one who did not 'know'. I replied that people were slandering her because of her love for me. My father, who did not want me to profit from those rumours, told me that they had been rife before our affair, and even before her marriage.

Having maintained a dignified façade at home for so long, he suddenly lost all restraint. When I failed to return home for several days he sent the house-maid to Marthe's with a note addressed to me, ordering me to come home at once or he would declare my absence to the police and charge Mme L. with corrupting a minor.

Marthe managed to keep up appearances, assumed an air of surprise and told the house-maid that she would give me the envelope next time I called. I returned home soon afterwards, furious that my age should make me so beholden to others. Neither my father nor my mother deigned to speak to me. I looked through the Civil Code, but could not find the articles relating to minors. Strangely enough, it did not occur to me that my conduct could have resulted in my being sent to a reform school. In the end, having failed to learn anything from the Civil Code, I looked up the word 'minor' in the large Larousse. I must have re-read the article ten times, but found nothing that was relevant to my case.

Next day, my father again did nothing to stop me going out.

For those interested in the motives of his strange conduct, I can summarize them in a few lines: he let me behave as I wished; then he was ashamed of letting me do so and tried to discourage me with threats; but he was more angry with himself than with me, and finally, shame at having lost his temper made him retract his prohibitions.

Mme Grangier's curiosity was aroused on her return from the coast by the neighbours' insidious questions. Pretending that they thought I was Jacques' brother, they told her all they knew of our activities. And as Marthe could not prevent herself talking about me at the slightest provocation, mentioning something I had done or said, her mother was not kept long in doubt as to the identity of Jacques' brother.

Believing that the child, which she assumed was Jacques', would put an end to the adventure, she decided to be lenient. She said nothing about it to M. Grangier, for fear of a scene. But she attributed this discretion to her own generosity of spirit, for which Marthe must be made to show due appreciation. To show her daughter that she knew everything, she harassed her unmercifully with hints and criticisms. But she did so in such a clumsy fashion that when M. Grangier was alone with his wife, he asked her to show more consideration for their poor, innocent child, who would go out of her mind if subjected to such continual suppositions. To which Mme Grangier replied with a smile that seemed to imply that Marthe had already admitted everything.

This attitude, and her previous attitude at the time of Jacques' first leave, led me to believe that Mme Grangier, even if she had disapproved entirely of her daughter's conduct, would have taken her side simply for the satisfaction of opposing her husband and son-in-law. In fact, Mme Grangier admired Marthe for betraying her husband; it was something that she herself, either because of moral scruples or simply because the opportunity had never arisen, had never dared to do. Her daughter, thought Mme Grangier, was revenging her for having been misunderstood. Foolish idealist that she was, her only regret was that Marthe should have fallen in love with a boy as young as me – less qualified than anyone to understand 'feminine sensibilities'.

The Lacombes, whom Marthe visited less and less, lived in Paris and could not therefore suspect anything. They simply found Marthe's behaviour increasingly strange and liked her less and less. They were worried about the future. They wondered what their son's marriage would be like in a few years' time. All mothers, on principle, wish for nothing so much as that their sons should get married, but they invariably disapprove of the women they choose. Jacques' mother felt sorry for her son that he should have such a wife. As for Mlle Lacombe, her spiteful attitude derived from the fact that Marthe alone held the secret of the idyll that had blossomed during the summer she had first met Jacques at the sea-side. The sister predicted the direst future for the marriage, saying that sooner or later Marthe would be unfaithful to Jacques, if, that is, she had not been so already.

His wife's and daughter's relentless persecution of Marthe sometimes made M. Lacombe, a simple, kindly fellow who was very fond of Marthe, leave the table. Mother and daughter then exchanged significant looks. In the case of Mme Lacombe this meant: 'You see, my dear, how women like that manage to bewitch our men.' Whereas Mlle Lacombe's expression meant: 'It's because I'm not like Marthe that I haven't found a husband.' In fact the poor girl, acting on the assumption that manners change with the times, and that marriages were no longer concluded in the old-fashioned way, frightened off prospective husbands by her lack of any spirit of resistance. Her marriage hopes lasted no longer than the summer season at a holiday resort. The young men promised to call as soon as they were back in Paris and ask for Mlle Lacombe's hand in marriage. But they were never seen again. Mlle Lacombe would soon be twenty-five and well on the way to becoming an old maid. So perhaps her main bone of contention was that Marthe should have found a husband so easily. She consoled herself with the thought that it was only her idiot of a brother who had been taken in by her.

Twenty-eight

Yet, whatever suspicions were entertained by the two families, no one imagined that the father of Marthe's child could be anyone but Jacques. This, I confess, rather vexed me. There were even days when I accused Marthe of cowardice for not revealing the truth. I was only too inclined to see in all around me the weakness that was really my own. So because Mme Grangier had avoided a scandal when she first learnt of our affair I assumed she would continue to turn a blind eye right up to the end.

The storm was blowing up. My father threatened to send certain letters to Mme Grangier. I hoped he would carry out his threats. On reflection I realized that Mme Grangier would not show the letters to her husband. In any case it was in the interests of both of them that the storm should not break. I was suffocating. I was crying for the storm. My father should send those letters direct to Jacques.

The day when he told me in anger that he had done so, I could have embraced him. At last! At last, I thought, he has done me the great service of telling Jacques what he ought to know. I pitied my father for thinking my love was so weak a thing. Moreover, these letters would at last put an end to Jacques' intolerable sentimentalizing over our child. I was too disturbed to realize how foolish, how utterly unthinkable this act would have been. I only began to see things more clearly when, the following day, my father, having recovered his accustomed calm, reassured me, as he thought, by admitting that he had done nothing of the kind. It would have been inhuman, he said. It would have been, of course. But at what point does the inhuman become the human?

I exhausted my nervous energy swinging between cowardice and boldness, suffering the innumerable contradictions inherent in the situation of a boy of my age attempting to come to grips with a man's adventure.

Twenty-nine

Love anaesthetized in me everything that did not pertain to Marthe. I did not think that I could be causing my father pain. My judgement was so distorted and so petty that I even came to the conclusion that war had been declared between us. It was not only out of love for Marthe that I contravened my filial duties, but sometimes, I am ashamed to admit, in a spirit of reprisal!

I no longer took much notice of the letters that my father sent round to Marthe's. Indeed, it was generally Marthe herself who begged me to go home more often and behave more reasonably. 'Are you too going to take sides against me?' I would cry, gritting my teeth, and stamping on the floor. That I should fly into such a state at the thought of being apart from her for a few hours, Marthe saw as a sign of passion. This certainty of being loved gave her a firmness that I had never seen in her before. Sure that I would be thinking of her the whole time, she insisted on my going home.

I soon realized where her courage came from. I began to change my tactics. I pretended to be convinced by her reasoning. Then, suddenly, her expression changed. Seeing me so reasonable (or so unconcerned), she began to fear that I loved her less. It was now she who wanted me to stay, so much did she need reassurance.

Yet on one occasion nothing would persuade me to go home. For three days I had not set foot in my parents' house, and I told

Marthe that I intended to spend another night with her. She did everything in her power to dissuade me: she covered me with kisses and when that failed she used threats. It was now her turn to bluff. In the end she declared that if I did not go home to my parents she would go to hers.

I replied that my father would be quite unmoved by such a gesture on her part. Well, then she wouldn't go home! She would go down to the Marne. She would catch a chill and die. She would then be rid of me at last. 'Have some pity for our child at least,' said Marthe. 'Don't compromise its future for such a trifle.' She accused me of playing with her love, of trying to test her to the utmost. In the face of such inflexible determination I repeated what my father had said about Marthe – that she was unfaithful to me with every man that came along – and said I was not going to be taken in. 'The only reason you won't give in,' I said, 'is because you're expecting one of your lovers.' What could she reply to such a foolish, unjust accusation? She turned away. I then reproached her for not vigorously denying the charge. At last my efforts were rewarded. She agreed to spend the night with me, on condition that we went somewhere else. She could not bear having the landlord say to the messenger from my parents the next morning that she was there.

But where could we spend the night?

We were like children standing on a chair, proud to be taller than the grown-ups. Circumstances had hoisted us up, but this did not make us adults. And if, in our experience, certain complicated things seemed very simple, other very simple things became serious obstacles. We had never dared to use Paul's flat in Paris. I did not think myself capable of slipping a coin into the concierge's hand and explaining that we would be coming there from time to time.

So the only alternative was a hotel. I had never been to a hotel before. The very idea of crossing the threshold of one terrified me.

Children are compelled to look for excuses. They are constantly being called upon to justify their actions before parents, so it is inevitable that they should lie.

I would have felt obliged to make excuses for myself even to a seedy-looking hotel boy. So I told Marthe that we would need some linen and various toilet requisites and made her pack a suit-case. We would ask for two rooms. They would think we were brother and sister. I would never dare to ask for one room for fear that my age (the age at which one is thrown out of casinos) should involve me in humiliation.

The journey, at eleven o'clock at night, seemed interminable. There were two other people in our carriage: a woman was accompanying her husband, a captain, to the Gare de l'Est. The train was neither lit nor heated. Marthe rested her head against the damp window. She had submitted to the cruel caprice of a young boy and had to endure the consequences. I felt ashamed at the thought of how much more Jacques, who was always so kind to her, deserved her love than I.

I could not help murmuring excuses. Marthe just shook her head. 'I would rather be unhappy with you than happy with him,' she whispered. One is almost ashamed to repeat such meaningless expressions of love, but in the mouth of the beloved they can set one's heart aflame. I even thought I understood Marthe's words. Yet what did they mean exactly? Can one be happy with somebody one does not love?

And I asked myself – I still ask myself – whether love gives one the right to snatch a woman from a fate which, although it may be mediocre, is at least peaceful. 'I would rather be unhappy with you . . .' – were these words an unconscious reproach? Because she loved me, Marthe had no doubt known times with me which, with Jacques, she would never have dreamt of. But did these moments of happiness give me the right to be cruel?

We got off the train at the Bastille. I can endure cold because for me it is the cleanest thing in the world, but the cold in that station was dirtier than the heat of a sea-port in summer, and without the compensating gaiety. Marthe complained of cramp. She clung to my arm. A lamentable couple we made, unaware of our youth and beauty and as ashamed of ourselves as if we had been a couple of beggars!

I was afraid that Marthe's obviously pregnant condition would look ridiculous and I walked with downcast eyes. At that moment I was far removed from any feelings of paternal pride.

We wandered in the icy rain from the Bastille to the Gare de Lyon. Every time we passed a hotel I made up some poor excuse for not going in and told Marthe that I was looking for something more suitable.

When we reached the Place de la Gare de Lyon, it became difficult to pretend any longer. Marthe begged me to put an end to this torture.

So, leaving Marthe outside, I plucked up enough courage to enter a fairly respectable-looking hotel. I had no idea what to expect. The reception-clerk asked me if I wanted a room. It would have been easy enough to say yes. Indeed, it was too easy and, looking for an excuse, as if I was a hotel thief surprised in the act, I asked to see Mme Lacombe. I blushed as I did so, half fearing that he might reply: 'Are you trying to be funny, young man? You know perfectly well she is outside in the street.' He looked through the list of residents. I must have got the wrong address. I came out and explained to Marthe that the hotel was full and that we would find no accommodation anywhere in the district. I sighed with relief. I was as anxious to get away as a thief on the run.

Up till then my concern to avoid the hotels to which I was

supposed to be taking Marthe against her will had been so overriding that I had not even considered Marthe herself. I now looked at her and her obvious distress almost moved me to tears. When she asked me where we would find a bed, I told her not to be too angry with me, that I must be out of my mind and that we should both be reasonable and go home – she to her flat at J. and I to my parents'. Out of my mind! Reasonable! She smiled a weak mechanical smile at the words.

The journey back was made all the more dramatic by my feelings of shame. When, after all she had endured, Marthe was rash enough to remark how unkind I had been, I lost my temper and accused her of lacking generosity. When, on the other hand, she was silent and seemed to have forgotten everything, I was afraid that it was because she really thought I was out of my mind. I went on at her then until I had made her say that she would never forget and that if she forgave me I must not take advantage of her clemency; that one day, exhausted by my ill treatment of her, her desire for peace would overcome her love and she would leave me. When I made her speak to me like this I experienced a delicious pain – even though I did not believe in the threats – rather like that aroused in me by the switchbacks at a fair, but stronger. I would then throw myself upon Marthe and embrace her more passionately than ever.

'Say that once again, that you'll leave me,' I panted, squeezing her in my arms as if I wanted to break her. Submissive to my will as no slave could be, but rather as a medium, she said over and over, just to please me, things of whose meaning she understood nothing.

Thirty

That night of the hotels was a turning-point in our relationship – though after so many other examples of my extravagant behaviour I was hardly aware of it. I may have thought that we could limp on forever like that, but Marthe, crouching in the corner of the carriage, exhausted, her teeth chattering with cold, had understood *everything*. She may even have seen that at the end of this year-long race, in this wildly driven carriage, there could be no other outcome but death.

Thirty-one

The following day I called on Marthe and found her, as usual, in bed. I wanted to join her, but she pushed me away gently. 'I don't feel very well,' she said. 'Go away. Don't come near me or you'll catch my cold.' She was coughing and she had a temperature. Smiling, so as not to seem too reproachful, she said she must have caught a chill the night before. Despite her anxiety she would not let me get the doctor. 'It's nothing really,' she said. 'All I need is to keep warm.' In fact, the reason why she did not want to have me go and fetch the doctor was that she did not want to compromise herself in the eyes of an old friend of the family. I needed to be reassured so badly that Marthe's refusal was enough to dissipate my anxiety. But it returned, even more strongly, when Marthe asked me to make a detour on my way home in order to take a letter to the doctor's.

When I arrived at Marthe's the following day I passed the doctor on the stairs. I dared not ask him how Marthe was, but I scrutinized his face. His air of calm reassured me, but it was no more than a professional mask.

I ran into the bedroom. It was empty. Where was Marthe? I then saw that her head was under the bedclothes. She was crying. The doctor had ordered her to stay in bed until the baby was born. Moreover, she would have to go to her parents'. She needed to be well looked after. We would be separated.

Misfortune never seems just. Only happiness is one's due. In accepting this misfortune without demur I was not being brave. It was simply that my mind could not encompass it. I listened, stupefied, to the doctor's decree, as a condemned man listens to his sentence being passed. If he does not flinch, people say how brave he is. It isn't bravery at all, but a failure of the imagination. He does not actually hear the sentence until they wake him on the morning of his execution. Similarly, I did not realize that we would not see each other again until the cab that the doctor had sent to take Marthe home arrived. The doctor had promised not to warn her parents, as Marthe had insisted on arriving unexpectedly.

I stopped the cab a short distance from the Grangiers' house. When the cabman turned round for the third time, we got out. He thought he had surprised us in the middle of our third kiss – but it was the same one. I left Marthe without making any arrangements to write to her, almost without saying goodbye, as if I would be seeing her again in an hour's time. Curious neighbours were already at their windows.

My mother noticed that my eyes were red. My sisters laughed because I twice dropped my soup spoon. The floor seemed to move beneath my feet. I had no sea-legs for pain. Indeed, this dizziness of the heart was more like sea-sickness than anything else I know of. Life without Marthe was a long crossing. Would it ever end? Just as during the first attacks of sea-sickness one loses all desire to reach one's destination and wants only to die on the spot, I thought little of the future. Some days later, when the sickness had become less violent, I had time to think once again of land.

There was little that Marthe's parents did not now know. They did not stop at intercepting my letters. They burned them in front of her, in her bedroom fire. Hers were scribbled in pencil and were scarcely legible. Her brother posted them.

*

I no longer had to face rows at home. In the evenings I sat with my father in front of the fire and resumed the conversations we used to have together. After this year I had become a stranger to my sisters. Gradually they got used to me again. I sat the youngest one on my knee and, in the darkness of the room, hugged her so violently that she tried to struggle free, half laughing and half crying. I thought of my own child, but it made me sad. It seemed impossible that I could feel more tenderly towards it. Was I old enough for a baby to be more to me than a brother or sister?

My father suggested distractions to me. Such suggestions come only from one who is calm. What could I do, other than what I could no longer do? I trembled at the sound of the door-bell or a passing cab. From within my prison walls I watched for the smallest sign of deliverance.

Straining my ears for sounds that might have some meaning intended for me, I heard one day the sound of bells. The armistice had been declared.

For me the armistice meant Jacques' return. I could picture him at Marthe's bedside, but I was helpless. I was lost.

My father was going back into Paris and wanted me to go with him. 'We can't miss an occasion like this,' he said. It would have seemed monstrous to refuse. And, in fact, my misery was such that I was not averse to witnessing the joy of others.

I must admit that I scarcely envied it. I thought that I alone was capable of experiencing those feelings that are attributed to a crowd. I looked around for signs of patriotic feeling. It was perhaps my injustice that saw only pleasure at an unexpected holiday: the cafés were open later and the soldiers could kiss the shop-girls. I had expected this sight to cause me pain, or make me jealous, or even to sweep me up in some great wave of emotion. In fact, it bored me.

Thirty-two

For some days there had been no letter. On one of the few afternoons when it snowed, my brothers brought me a message delivered by young Grangier. It was an icy letter from Mme Grangier, asking me to come as soon as possible. What could she want with me? The opportunity of being in some sort of contact, however indirect, with Marthe, outweighed my fears. I imagined Mme Grangier forbidding me to see her daughter again, or to write to her, and me standing there, head bowed like a schoolboy who has been caught out. I would be incapable of losing my temper and saying what I wanted to say. No gesture of mine would betray my hatred. I would politely take my leave and the door would be shut behind me for ever. Only then would I think of all the replies, the clever arguments, the cutting words that might have left Mme Grangier a less pitiful image of her daughter's lover than that of a misbehaving schoolboy. I could foresee the scene, second by second.

When I entered the small sitting-room, I seemed to be reliving my first visit. So this visit meant that I would perhaps never see Marthe again.

Mme Grangier appeared. I could not help but feel sorry for her on account of her short stature, for she was doing her best to behave in a haughty manner towards me. She apologized for having brought me there for nothing. She had sent me the message, she claimed, because she wanted some information that was too complicated to explain by letter, but in the meantime she had found what she had been looking for. This absurd mystery caused me more torment than any catastrophe would have done.

Down by the Marne I met young Grangier, leaning against some railings. He had been hit in the face with a snowball and was crying. I tried to comfort him, and asked him about Marthe. He told me that his sister had been calling out for me. Their mother would not hear of it, but their father had said: 'Marthe is very ill. She must not be contradicted.'

I understood at once Mme Grangier's strange, very bourgeois behaviour towards me. Out of respect for her husband and for the wishes of someone about to die, she had sent for me. But when the danger had passed and Marthe was better again, the order was cancelled. I should have been happy. Instead, I regretted that the danger had not lasted long enough to allow me to see the invalid.

Two days later I received a letter from Marthe. She made no mention of my visit. She had probably not been told that I had come. She talked about our future in a different, serene almost celestial way that rather disturbed me. Is it true perhaps that love is the most violent form of selfishness? For, when I tried to find the reason why it had disturbed me, I discovered that I was jealous of our child, because now Marthe spoke more about the child than about me.

We were expecting the child in March. One Friday in January my brothers came rushing into the house and breathlessly announced that young Grangier had a nephew. I could not understand their triumphant air, nor why they had run so fast. They could certainly not have any idea of how important this news was to me. I realized later that for them an uncle was always old, so it was something of a miracle that young Grangier should have become one. They had run home to share their astonishment.

It is the object that we see before us every day which, when it is moved from its usual place, we find most difficult to recognize. I did not at first recognize young Grangier's nephew as Marthe's child – my child.

There was a short-circuit in the lighting; the audience was thrown into a panic – and I was the theatre where this was taking place. Suddenly it was quite dark inside me: my feelings collided with each other and I groped around for dates and facts to cling on to. I counted on my fingers as I had seen Marthe do – though at the time I never suspected any deception. But this exercise did not help me in the least. I had forgotten how to count. How could this child that was expected in March be born in January? All the explanations I found for this abnormality were the product of jealousy. Then, suddenly, the certainty dawned on me that the child must be Jacques'. Had he not been home on leave exactly nine months before? This meant that Marthe had been lying to me ever since. In any case, she had already lied to me about Jacques' leave! Hadn't she sworn to me that she had refused to sleep with Jacques throughout the whole terrible fortnight, only to admit, much later, that he had taken her on several occasions!

I had never thought very seriously that this child might be Jacques'. When Marthe had first told mc that she was pregnant I had, in my cowardice, wished that it had been. But having lived for several months with the inevitable, borne up by the certainty that I was the father, I had come to love this child – this child that was not, it seemed, mine at all. Why must I finally achieve the feelings of a father only at the moment of learning that I was not one?

It is obvious that my mind was in an incredible state of disarray. It was as if I had been thrown into a river on a dark night, not knowing how to swim. One thing above all I could not understand, and that was Marthe's audacity in calling this legitimate child after me. At times I saw this as a gesture of defiance against a fate that had refused to allow the child to be mine. At others I saw it simply as a lack of tact, one of those lapses of taste which had often surprised me in Marthe, but which were simply the result of an excess of love.

I had begun a letter of abuse. I felt I owed it to my own self-respect! But the words would not come; my thoughts were elsewhere, in more noble regions of the heart.

I tore up the letter and wrote another in which I expressed what I really felt. I asked Marthe's forgiveness. For what? Probably because her son was not mine. I begged her to love me all the same.

A very young man is an animal that does not take easily to suffering. I was already re-arranging my views of the situation. I had almost come to accept the child as not being mine. But before I had finished the letter I received one from Marthe. She was overcome with joy this son was ours, born two months early. He had had to be put in an incubator. 'I nearly died,' she said. The phrase amused me by its childishness.

I had no room in my heart for any other emotion but joy. I wanted to share the news of this birth with the whole world and to tell my brothers that they too were uncles. From the heights of my joy I looked down with contempt on my earlier suspicions. How could I ever have doubted Marthe? This remorse, mingled with my new-found happiness, made me love Marthe – and my son – more than ever. In my incoherence I was grateful that for a few brief moments I had known what it was to suffer – for so I thought. But nothing is less like a thing than that which is closest to it. A man who has been near to death thinks he knows death. When the day finally comes for him to meet it, he does not recognize it. 'This is not it,' he says, as he dies.

In her letter Marthe said: 'He is like you.' I had seen my brothers and sisters just after they were born and I knew that only love can show a woman the resemblance she is searching for. 'He has my eyes,' she added. Again only her desire to see us united in a single being could make her recognize her own eyes in the child's.

The Grangiers were no longer in any doubt. But whatever their feelings towards Marthe, they wished at all costs to avoid a scandal that would involve the whole family. So they became her accomplices. The doctor, too, was an accomplice in the cause of public decency. He agreed to conceal the fact that the birth had been premature and to explain away, to the husband's satisfaction, the need for an incubator.

It seemed perfectly natural during the next few days that no further word should come from Marthe. Jacques was probably at her bedside. On no previous occasion had Jacques' presence affected me less. I felt no resentment that he should have been given leave for the birth of 'his' son. In a last access of childishness, I even smiled at the thought that he owed his leave to me.

Thirty-three

At home, an air of calm reigned over the whole house.

True presentiments are formed at a level of our minds unvisited by reason. Thus it is that, sometimes, they make us perform actions that we interpret quite wrongly.

I thought that I owed my new-found tenderness to my happiness and I was pleased to know that Marthe was in a house that my happy memories transformed into a fetish.

A disorderly man who is about to die, and does not know it, suddenly begins to put everything around him in order. His life changes. He files his papers. He rises early and retires early to bed. He gives up his vices. His friends are pleased with the change that has come over him. As a result, his sudden death seems all the more unjust. *He was going to have a happy life*.

Similarly, the regularity of my new life was merely the final preparation of a condemned man. I thought that I was a better son because I had one of my own. But, in fact, I felt more tenderly towards father and mother because something inside me knew that, before long, I would need all their tenderness.

One day, at lunch-time, my brothers came running in from school shouting that Marthe was dead.

When lightning strikes a man it kills so quickly that he feels nothing. It is his companion who is affected by the sight.

Whereas I felt nothing, my father's face was distorted with pain. He pushed my brothers out of the room. 'Go away! Go away! You must be mad!' he stammered. I felt myself becoming hard, cold, like a stone. Then, just as a dying man may relive the experiences of a lifetime in a single second, I saw my love for the first time as a whole, with all its aberrations. Because my father was crying, I too burst into tears. My mother then took charge of me. Dry-eyed, she nursed me coldly, tenderly, for all the world as if I had had scarlet fever.

At first, my fainting fit was a sufficient reason why my brothers had to be quiet in the house. But they could not understand why this silence had to be maintained for days on end. They had never been forbidden to play noisy games. However, they kept very quiet. But their footsteps on the tiled floor of the hall at midday made me lose consciousness as if, each time, they had come to tell me that Marthe was dead.

Marthe! My jealousy pursued her to the grave and I hoped that there was nothing after death. In the same way we cannot bear the person we love to go without us to some gathering where there will be a lot of people. My heart was at an age when one does not yet think of the future. Yes, what I wished for Marthe was oblivion, rather than a new world where one day I might join her.

Thirty-four

The only time I ever saw Jacques was a few months later. He knew that my father had some of Marthe's watercolours and he wanted to see them. We are always anxious to discover more about those we love. I wanted to see the man to whom Marthe had given her hand.

Holding my breath, I tip-toed over to the half-open door. I arrived in time to hear him say:

'My wife called out his name just before she died. Poor child! He's all I have to live for.'

Seeing this widower striving to maintain a stoic calm and to master his despair, I realized that in the end order reasserts itself over everything. Had I not just learnt that Marthe had died calling my name, and that my son would have a reasonable life?

Afterword

Of all the first novels launched into best-sellerdom this century with the aid of modern publicity and sales methods, few have survived the tests of changing taste and passing time for even a decade. Raymond Radiguet's *The Devil in the Flesh*, which was published in 1923 to the accompaniment of unprecedented ballyhoo, is one of the rare exceptions to the rule: it still commands both popular admiration and critical esteem.

Its author was born at Parc Saint-Maur, a few miles outside Paris, on 18 June 1903, the son of the artist and cartoonist Maurice Radiguet. The eldest of seven children, he spent an unremarkable childhood in the suburbs, playing with his brothers and sisters, working well at the local primary school, and eventually passing the scholarship examination to the Lycée Charlemagne in Paris. About this time, however, a change occurred in his character and behaviour, which foreshadowed his future development: he occasionally became withdrawn at home, neglected his studies, played truant from school, and took to spending his days in the family boat on the Marne, reading books from his father's library. These included eighteenth-century *contes*, Symbolist poetry, and novels by such masters of amorous psychology as Madame de Lafayette and Stendhal.

At the age of fifteen he had his first and most significant love-affair, which he was later to use as the basis for *The Devil in the*

Flesh. He also appeared in print for the first time, when *Le Canard enchaîné* printed one of his poems. He showed some other poems, signed with the exotic pseudonym Rajki, to André Salmon, to whom he had to deliver his father's cartoons every day for the newspaper *L'Intransigeant*. Salmon was impressed by their 'exquisite sobriety', and not only told the boy sternly that 'no poet could decently call himself Rajki' but offered to help him to find work as a journalist. Radiguet promptly decided to abandon his studies in order to devote himself entirely to journalism and literature.

Within a short time he was in the midst of the maelstrom which was literary and artistic life in Paris at the end of the First World War. Among the writers and painters he met were Max Jacob, Blaise Cendrars, Pierre Reverdy, Picasso and Modigliani, but the encounter which did most to shape his life and work was that with Jean Cocteau. He was introduced to Cocteau at an art-gallery one evening, and a few days later the poet's valet informed him that there was 'a child with a walking-stick' waiting to see him. The 'child' was anything but a prepossessing figure. 'He was small, pale-faced, and short-sighted,' Cocteau wrote later, 'with badly cut hair hanging over his collar and giving him side-whiskers. He kept pulling faces as if he were in the sun, and hopped about as he walked . . . From his pockets he pulled little pages from a school exercise book which he had screwed up into a ball . . . If he wanted to examine a picture or a text, he took out of his pocket some broken spectacles which he used as a monocle . . .' But the poems the fifteen-year-old read out from his crumpled pieces of paper convinced Cocteau that his visitor was a genius. He not only gave him encouragement and help, but, in his own words, 'chose him as a son'. Soon the two of them – the elegant, elfin prince of letters and the awkward, sullen boy – were inseparable companions.

Together they produced a comic opera with Erik Satie, founded a literary review which lasted six months, and presented *The Pelicans*, a comedy which was the only play Radiguet ever wrote. At first Radiguet had continued to live at Parc Saint-Maur, returning home every night by the last train. Soon, however, he took to staying in friends' studios or cheap hotel rooms in the Madeleine district, and more often than not he would spend all night with Cocteau and his friends in some bar. For some months the group met at the *Gaya*, a bar in the rue Duphot kept by Louis Moysés, and they followed Moysés when he moved to the rue Boissy d'Anglas and opened the famous *Bœuf sur le toit*.

Here Radiguet could nearly always be found sitting with Cocteau, smoking and drinking heavily, but holding himself aloof from the dancing and conversation all around him. His silence and reserve were generally interpreted as signs of precocity and an intense inner life, but they were more probably the results of a paralysing shyness and a morbid awareness of his own youthfulness. He loved the idea of ageing, according to Cocteau, and where others said: 'When I was young,' he would say: 'When I am old . . .' Certainly he convinced many of his companions that he was old beyond his years; Camille Aymard wrote of him: 'He was a child with no youth, no exuberance, no illusions. He reminded me of those young Chinese scholars who, at twenty, wear on their timeless masks an expression of precocious old age.'

Whether his *gravitas* was a mark of maturity or a mask for youthful timidity, Radiguet found it impossible to write anything of value in the bohemian atmosphere of post-war Paris. It was only on holiday with Cocteau that he succeeded in producing work that satisfied him. Thus at Carqueiranne, in April 1920, he wrote the poems which, together with the verse he had written at Parc Saint-Maur, would make up the collection *Cheeks on Fire*. Then, the following year, in the little fishing village of Piquey, near Arcachon, he turned to a new genre and wrote the novel which was to bring him fame, *The Devil in the Flesh*.

He had, in fact, sketched out the early episodes of this book in 1919, but it was not until the summer of 1921 that he found the peace he required to complete the novel. Even so, he was torn between what Cocteau called 'the certainty of working wonders and the bad-tempered laziness of a schoolboy', and his friends sometimes had to lock him in his hotel room to force him to work. Cocteau also repeatedly urged his pupil in the direction in which he considered his genius lay, however unfashionable it might be: towards greater simplicity. 'Raymond, be commonplace,' he would exhort him; 'Raymond, write like everyone else.' With the result that Radiguet wrote like no one else of his time, in a sober, simple, unadorned style.

By the time the group returned to Paris, *The Devil in the Flesh* was finished, and Cocteau delivered it to *La Sirène* for publication. In the meantime he tried to find Radiguet an official sinecure, and recommended the boy as 'a miracle, not a prodigy' to Philippe Berthelot at the Foreign Ministry. 'He has just written a novel,' he told Berthelot, 'which I consider *one of the four or five masterpieces of French literature.*' In the event, however, it was not the Foreign Ministry which provided Radiguet with a guaranteed living, but the publisher Bernard Grasset. When negotiations with *La Siréne* broke down, Cocteau took Radiguet and the novel to Grasset's office in the rue des Saints-Pères and read out the first pages in the presence of the author, whom the publisher later remembered 'looking like a schoolboy at his first interview with the headmaster'. Grasset was enthusiastic about the book, accepted it for publication, and signed a contract giving Radiguet a monthly allowance of 1,500 francs. His only criticism was that the novel lacked a proper conclusion, and Radiguet accordingly rewrote the last chapters of *The Devil in the Flesh*, which he read to his friends at the end of March 1922.

There seemed to be no reason why the novel should not be published by the end of the year, but it did not appear on the bookstalls until March 1923. The reason for the delay was that Grasset had decided to launch the book with a publicity campaign on a scale hitherto unknown in France. Explaining his methods some years later, he wrote that although he had recognized Radiguet's genius, his publicity for *The Devil in the Flesh* had dealt only incidentally with his literary gifts: 'I did not say: "I have found a great novelist," I simply said: "I have discovered a seventeen-year-old author." In my opinion this fact was likely to arouse the public's curiosity. Once the book had been widely distributed and read, as a result of that curiosity, the public realized that it was a great work, and it then became possible to talk of the author's gifts.'

As might have been expected, Grasset's campaign provoked a violent adverse reaction from the critics. They protested at the puffing of a novel as if it were a hair-restorer or a patent medicine, but above all at the insistence on Radiguet's extreme youth. 'For my part,' wrote one critic, 'I don't care whether the author is seventeen or a hundred and seven. It is a book we have to judge, not a birth certificate.' Others, however, argued that at seventeen no author could have sufficient experience of life to write a novel of any merit, let alone a masterpiece; and a humorist in one paper (who may have lived to witness the success of little Minou Drouet) invented an eight-year-old authoress called Zozo, signing a contract for ten years and lispingly explaining that at eighteen she would be 'too old to go on writing'. Radiguet thought it necessary to reply to this objection, which he did in an article in *Les Nouvelles littéraires* on publication day. After defending Grasset's publicity campaign, he chided those who criticized his book solely on the ground of his age:

It is a truism, and consequently a truth, not to be lightly dismissed, that in order to write, one must have lived. But what I would like to know is at what age one is entitled to say: 'I have lived.' Doesn't this use of the past tense logically imply death? For my part, I think that at any age, even the earliest, one has both lived and is beginning to live. Be that as it may, it does not strike me as unduly impertinent to assert our right to use memories of our first years before our last years have arrived. Not that we would condemn the potent charm of speaking of the dawn in the evening of a beautiful day, but, however different it may be, there is no less interest in speaking of the dawn without waiting for nightfall.

In fact, after reading the novel, even those critics who had been loudest in their protests at Grasset's publicity methods admitted its merits. Frédéric Lefèvre spoke for nearly all his colleagues when he drew attention to 'the highly amusing contrast between the rather noisy way in which this work has been launched and its intrinsic qualities: restraint, freshness, distinction'. The public, for their part, had no doubts, and *The Devil in the Flesh* became a runaway best-seller. Only one section of the population remained resolutely hostile to the novel: the men who had fought in the trenches during the war. They illogically but very naturally regarded Radiguet's story of the love-affair between a schoolboy and a soldier's wife as an insult to the French Army; and when an American literary prize was awarded to the novel, the Association of War Veteran Writers sent a cable to the American Legion protesting at this tribute to a work which 'deeply wounded the feelings of all war veterans'. A more personal reproach to Radiguet came in a letter to him from Roland Dorgelès, author of *The Wooden Crosses*, a war novel written from the soldier's view-point. After thanking Radiguet for sending him a copy of *The Devil in the Flesh*, he wrote that he hesitated to praise the 'real talent' the book revealed, and went on: 'This is because, from the first page to the last, it shows a complete lack of feelings, and if I am happily surprised that you should have been able to write such a book at twenty, I am distressed that you should have conceived it at that age . . .' As we shall see, because of his special position in the affections of the *poilus*, Dorgelès would unwittingly find himself playing a further part in the Radiguet story thirty years later.

The success of *The Devil in the Flesh* transformed the material side of Radiguet's life: he moved into Foyot's, opposite the Luxembourg, entertained lavishly, dressed elegantly. In the summer of 1923 he left for Arcachon once more, to spend his holidays with Cocteau and his friends at Piquey. There an astonishing change took place in his behaviour. He forswore alcohol and late nights and applied himself to his work, finishing his second novel, *Count Orgel's Ball*, and arranging his poems in a collection. It was as if he had a premonition of his approaching death, and his friends were painfully reminded a few months later of the passage towards the end of *The Devil in the Flesh*:

> An untidy man who is about to die but does not suspect it, suddenly puts everything around him in order. His life changes. He sorts out his papers. He gets up early, goes to bed early, and gives up his vices. Those around him rejoice, so that his brutal death seems all the more unjust. *He was about to lead a happy life.*

Soon after returning to Paris in late October, Radiguet fell ill with typhoid fever, but although he was obviously a sick man he refused to take medical advice. By the time he was forced to take to his bed, and the doctors were called in, it was too late. During the last weeks of his life the mask of arrogance which had taken in so many onlookers fell away, and the shy boy Cocteau had befriended five years before reappeared. Joseph

Kessel, who brought him the proofs of *Count Orgel's Ball*, later recalled that 'When he saw the bundle of printed sheets I was holding, there appeared in his short-sighted eyes, at once vague and piercing, pale and deep, a sort of eager inquiry. How far he was from that haughty detachment, that pride and self-assurance, which people attributed to him!' And an hour before he died, he turned to his father and said: 'If you only knew how much and how deeply I love you . . .'

On 9 December 1923, to use Cocteau's felicitous phrase, 'Raymond Radiguet began.' Cocteau, who was present at Radiguet's death, was heartbroken, and cynics nicknamed the 'widowed' poet *le veuf sur le toit*. 'Maritain will tell you how distressed I am,' he wrote to Henri Massis. 'For the past five years I had renounced myself. Through Radiguet I was trying an experiment which my filthy instruments would have prevented me from bringing off alone . . . I am suffering; I am left weak and powerless in the midst of a mortal emptiness, on the ruins of a crystal factory . . .'

There remained nothing for Radiguet's friends to do but to see his last works through the press, and then to defend his reputation against allegations that his posthumous publications had been touched up or even entirely written by Cocteau. *Count Orgel's Ball* won universal acclaim when it appeared in the summer of 1924, and although the critics had reservations about Radiguet's remaining poems, which were published in 1925, his fame was now secure. During the succeeding years his novels were reprinted at frequent intervals, and sales of *The Devil in the Flesh* increased enormously after 1947, when Gérard Philippe appeared in a film version of the book. Then, in 1954, came the revelation of a small private tragedy lasting thirty years which had been brought about by Radiguet's first novel.

In his preface to *Count Orgel's Ball*, Cocteau had published a document concerning *The Devil in the Flesh* which had been 'found among Radiguet's papers.' It read as follows:

People have insisted on regarding my book as a confession. What nonsense! Priests are well acquainted with this mechanism of the soul, which can be observed in young boys and women, of the false confession, in which a person admits to crimes he has not committed, out of pride. It is firstly to give *The Devil in the Flesh* the texture of a novel, and secondly to portray the character of the young boy who is the hero, that everything in the book is false. This boasting is part of the boy's character.

Thirty years later, Roland Dorgelès revealed that this document, which Radiguet had significantly not published during his lifetime, and which was manifestly untruthful in its assertion that 'everything in the book is false', had been made public only at the request of the ex-soldier husband of the original Marthe. This man had written to Dorgelès, the spokesman of the Great War veterans, in 1952, asking for an interview, and when they met he had burst into tears, explaining: 'I am the husband of the heroine of *The Devil in the Flesh*.' Two years later, in October 1954, he died of leukaemia, aged fifty-nine. He left Dorgelès a neatly wrapped parcel which contained an annotated copy of Radiguet's novel, together with the following letter:

Monsieur and Dear Comrade,

When you receive this letter I shall have joined Her whom I loved and who always loved me.

The cycle of our sorrows has thus ended, and I hope that oblivion will thrust into the void this novel which has done us so much harm.

You can, if you consider it necessary, publish the statement I have entrusted to you, using, if you think fit, the notes attached to the novel.

With the renewed assurance of my profound gratitude, I beg you to accept this expression of my sincerest regards as a former *poilu*.

Attached to this letter was the following statement:

I have an urgent duty to fulfil: I wish to see honour paid to the memory of Her who was made the heroine of this novel.

She was my wife, for She died not long ago.

Carried off at the age of fifty-nine by a cruel illness, her swift, brutal death has left me with the bitter after-taste of having occasionally doubted her love: 'Slander away! Something always remains.'

'It isn't true! I didn't do anything wrong!' Those were her last words. How often she repeated those two short sentences to me when I felt disheartened!

So, spurning the spiteful hypotheses of those who do not know or pretend not to know, I have decided to shed light on this drama and proclaim the truth.

She was a schoolteacher, born on 2 December 1893, and consequently aged between twenty-four and twenty-five at the time in which the events related in the novel take place.

R. Radiguet, born in 1903, was between fourteen and fifteen at the same time: a kid!

Her doctor had introduced her to the artist Radiguet in order to help her find the means of exhibiting some decorated pottery She had made.

Moreover, giving a few private lessons to R.K., a friend of R. Radiguet, She met the latter and observed that he possessed certain literary gifts which She decided to develop. This was the purpose of lessons given free of charge and when the occasion presented itself: She was a born Teacher who loved her profession. R. Radiguet thus came to know of a private Diary kept by my Wife.

Since 1914 (when I had left for the front) She had been in the habit of keeping a daily record of her thoughts and her life, a record which She gave me every time I came home on leave.

The Diary which R. Radiguet read covered the period from August 1917 to October 1918.

Now, that Diary disappeared!

It served as the plot for the novel *The Devil in the Flesh*, for the events we lived through, She and I, are to be found in that novel.

Naturally they have been altered and moved about, but they are clearly recognizable: the Sénart forest, the rue de Lyon, leaves, the mother-in-law's visit, etc.

He was a very intelligent boy, lazy and unscrupulous, with a sickly imagination.

The Devil in the Flesh has no preface. As soon as it came out, we read it: the result was a statement which Monsieur Cocteau inserted in the preface to *Count Orgel's Ball*.

This statement attributes the adventures of the hero of *The Devil in the Flesh* to a wild and childish imagination.

If one studies that book, one senses that it is incomplete; very detailed at the beginning, it speeds up towards the end. For anyone in the know, that is very understandable, since the sources of inspiration were lacking, my Wife's Diary stopping as it did in October 1918.

P.S. My Son's christian name is not Raymond.

If this document was pathetic, the annotations on the attached copy of *The Devil in the Flesh* were heartrending. 'Jacques' had spent thirty years in agonized exegesis of the hated text which had ruined his life, and sheets of paper inserted between the pages bore commentaries which read like cries of pain. Thus where Marthe begs her lover to bite her and mark her so that everyone may know, the husband wrote: '*This is what She used to say to me . . .*' Where the narrator tells how Marthe used to toss her husband's letters unopened into the fire, 'Jacques' retorted: '*I found all my letters again, like hers, except for a few he had stolen from us.*' Where the novel refers to a picnic in the Sénart forest, the husband's comment reads: '*This corresponds to the Écouen woods in September 1917, when the infantry division was resting. Before our wedding (17 October 1917).'* And where the adolescent hero claims that 'It was I who dictated to his wife the only tender letters he ever received from her,' the husband retorted in an angry note: '*See our letters – since 1914.*'

Wherever the husband found a discrepancy of fact in the novel, he seized on it with pathetic relief. For example, at the point where Radiguet tells how Marthe would row the boat, with the schoolboy's head resting in her lap, he wrote triumphantly: '*She could not row and did not like the water.*' Again, opposite the page on which Marthe hands her lover a pair of pyjamas belonging to her husband, 'Jacques' commented: '*I had no pyjamas.*' But more often his annotations confirmed the accuracy of the details given in the novel, while insisting that they had been copied from his letters, his wife's diary, and her letters which he returned to her whenever he came home on leave.

Both the husband's posthumous statement and his commentary on *The Devil in the Flesh* asserted his belief in his wife's innocence, which she herself protested throughout her married life and on her very deathbed. But even without his admission to Dorgelès that he had 'occasionally' queried her word, it is clear that he was tormented by doubt even before the publication of Radiguet's novel, and that *The Devil in the Flesh* only added fuel to his suspicions. For the child which his wife bore at the end of the war was put to nurse immediately after birth and left with the nurse for five years, even though the boy was crippled with poliomyelitis at the age of eighteen months. When he was five, his parents took him home, but four years later he was once again abandoned to the care of a nurse. 'I behaved badly towards the child,' the husband admitted to Dorgelès. 'I kept him away from the time he was born. I gave him no education. His sister, on the other hand, who was born a year later, was given a good upbringing: I had her properly educated . . .'

Not only did the husband spurn the first child of their marriage, but he and his wife left their house for another, before fleeing from the village where every glance seemed an accusation and every whisper a gibe. Again and again they moved house, travelling from one suburban district to another in their hopeless flight from rumour and doubt.

At last, after another world war, and with the approach of old age, they attained an uneasy peace. But then, in 1947, the hated book was turned into a film, with the part of the adolescent lover played by the darling of the French cinema, and Jacques was deceived again every night on every screen in the country. 'Then,' the husband told Dorgelès, 'it began all over again . . .'

The agony of these last years is shown in all its horror in a photograph I have seen of 'Marthe' towards the end of her life: a drawn, haggard face with wide eyes fixed in a terrible stare. Now only death could bring her peace, leaving her husband to endure two more years of mingled doubt and remorse. His life had been scarred and twisted by a book, yet when he died he asked for a book to be buried with him, as if to assert the power of literature to heal as well as hurt. This book, which was placed in his coffin together with his wife's drawings and some letters, was Dorgelès's *The Wooden Crosses*, the soldier's novel which had comforted him in the pain inflicted by a civilian.

Now, years later, it is as futile to sympathize with the original Jacques and Marthe of *The Devil in the Flesh* as it is to deplore Radiguet's early death. Pity, indignation, topicality, regret have all become irrelevant, and we are left with only the book to read and judge. Most critics today repeat the verdict of their predecessors: that the novel is a little masterpiece. It expresses all the anguish, joy and misery of adolescence, observed with cruel, unsentimental perspicuity, and recorded in a style of classic simplicity. It was written by a child, but as François Mauriac said of him, 'That child was a master.'

Robert Baldick

BEYOND GOOD AND EVIL

Friedrich Nietzsche

'That which is done out of love always takes place beyond good and evil'

Beyond Good and Evil confirmed Nietzsche's position as the towering European philosopher of his age. The work dramatically rejects traditional Western thought with its notions of truth and God, good and evil. Nietzsche seeks to demonstrate that the Christian world is steeped in a false piety and infected with a 'slave morality'. With wit and energy, he turns from this critique to a philosophy that celebrates the present and demands that the individual impose their own 'will to power' upon the world.

Translated by R. J. Hollingdale
With an Introduction by Michael Tanner

ISBN: 978 0 14 044 923 5

THE PICTURE OF DORIAN GRAY

Oscar Wilde

'The horror, whatever it was, had not yet entirely spoiled that marvellous beauty'

Enthralled by his own exquisite portrait, Dorian Gray exchanges his soul for eternal youth and beauty. Influenced by his friend Lord Henry Wotton, he is drawn into a corrupt double life, indulging his desires in secret while remaining a gentleman in the eyes of polite society. Only his portrait bears the traces of his decadence. *The Picture of Dorian Gray* was a *succès de scandale*. Early readers were shocked by its hints at unspeakable sins, and the book was later used as evidence against Wilde at his trial at the Old Bailey in 1895.

Edited with an introduction and notes by Robert Mighall

ISBN: 978 0 14 143 957 0

HEART OF DARKNESS

Joseph Conrad

'The horror! The horror!'

Marlow, a seaman and wanderer, recounts his physical and psychological journey in search of the infamous ivory trader Kurtz. Travelling up river to the heart of the African continent, he gradually becomes obsessed by this enigmatic, wraith-like figure. Marlow's discovery of how Kurtz has gained his position of power over the local people involves him in a radical questioning, not only of his own nature and values, but those of Western civilization. A haunting and hugely influential Modernist masterpiece, *Heart of Darkness* explores the limits of human experience as well as the nightmarish realities of imperialism.

Heart of Darkness edited with an Introduction by
Owen Knowles
Congo Diary edited with Notes by Robert Hampson
General editor J. H. Stape

ISBN: 978 0 14 144 167 2

THE AGE OF INNOCENCE

Edith Wharton

When the Countess Ellen Olenska returns from Europe, fleeing her brutish husband, her rebellious independence and passionate awareness of life stir the educated sensitivity of Newland Archer, already engaged to be married to the Countess's cousin May Welland. As the consequent drama unfolds, Edith Wharton's sharp ironic wit and Jamesian mastery of form create a disturbingly accurate picture of men and women caught in a society that denies humanity while desperately defending 'civilization'.

With an Introduction by Cynthia Griffin Wolff and Notes by Laura Dluzynski Quinn

ISBN: 978 0 14 018 970 4

A PASSAGE TO INDIA

E. M. Forster

'Shrines are fascinating, especially when rarely opened'

When Adela and her elderly companion Mrs Moore arrive in the Indian town of Chandrapore, they quickly feel trapped by its insular and prejudiced British community. Determined to explore the 'real India', they seek the guidance of the charming and mercurial Dr Aziz, a cultivated Indian Muslim. But a mysterious incident occurs when they are exploring the Marabar caves with Aziz, and the well-respected doctor soon finds himself at the centre of a scandal that rouses violent passions among both the British and their Indian subjects. A masterly portrait of a society in the grip of imperialism, *A Passage to India* compellingly depicts the fate of individuals caught in the great political and cultural conflicts of the modern world.

Edited by Oliver Stallybrass
With an Introduction by Pankaj Mishra

ISBN: 978 0 14 144 116 0

THE GARDEN PARTY

Katherine Mansfield

'Kisses, voices, tinkling spoons, laughter, the smell of crushed grass'

Innovative, startlingly perceptive and aglow with colour, these fifteen stories were written towards the end of Katherine Mansfield's tragically short life. Many are set in the author's native New Zealand, others in England and the French Riviera. All are revelations of the unspoken, half-understood emotions that make up everyday experience – from the blackly comic 'The Daughters of the Late Colonel', and the short, sharp sketch 'Miss Brill', in which a lonely woman's precarious sense of self is brutally destroyed, to the vivid, impressionistic evocation of family life in 'At the Bay' and the poignant, haunting miniature masterpiece 'The Garden Party'.

Edited with an Introduction and Notes by Lorna Sage

ISBN: 978 0 14 144 180 1

THE MASTER AND MARGARITA

Mikhail Bulgakov

'Manuscripts don't burn'

One spring afternoon the Devil, trailing fire and chaos in his wake, weaves himself out of the shadows and into Moscow in Bulgakov's fantastical, funny and frightening satire of Soviet life. Brimming with magic and incident, it is full of imaginary, historical, terrifying and wonderful characters, from witches, poets and Biblical tyrants to the beautiful and courageous Margarita, who will do anything to save the imprisoned writer she loves. Written in secret during the darkest days of Stalin's reign, when *The Master and Margarita* was finally published it became an overnight literary phenomenon, signalling artistic freedom for Russians everywhere.

Translated by Richard Pevear and Larissa Volokhonsky
With an Introduction by Richard Pevear

ISBN: 978 0 14 045 546 5

COUSIN BETTE

Honoré de Balzac

'Envy remained hidden in her heart, like a plague germ which may come to life and devestate the city'

Poor, plain spinster Bette is compelled to survive on the condescending patronage of her socially superior relatives in Paris: her beautiful, saintly cousin Adeline, the philandering Baron Hulot and their daughter Hortense. Already deeply resentful of their wealth, when Bette learns that the man she is in love with plans to marry Hortense, she becomes consumed by the desire to exact her revenge and dedicates herself to the destruction of the Hulot family, plotting their ruin with patient, silent malice. *Cousin Bette* is a gripping tale of violent jealousy, sexual passion and treachery, and a brilliant portrayal of the grasping, bourgeois society of 1840s Paris. The culmination of the *Comédie humaine,* Balzac's epic chronicle of his times, it is one of his greatest triumphs as a novelist.

Translated with an introduction by Marion Ayton Crawford

ISBN: 978 0 14 044 160 4